The First Degree

by

David Wayne Hillery

DORRANCE PUBLISHING CO., INC.
PITTSBURGH, PENNSYLVANIA 15222

ISBN: 978-1-4349-0473-7
Printed in the United States of America

First Printing

For more information or to order additional books, please contact:
Dorrance Publishing Co., Inc.
701 Smithfield Street
Pittsburgh, Pennsylvania 15222
U.S.A.
1-800-788-7654
www.dorrancebookstore.com

Part 1 – Someone Else's Mission

Chapter 1 – The First Gup

Something was about to begin. Everything was normal. I was coming home from work that day. As I entered onto the highway in my Toyota Camry, I began to pray, as usual, for God to protect me in the traffic. Most people probably don't consider their daily activities to be dangerous, but I considered hurtling through space on a concrete pavement in the immediate vicinity of dozens of other vehicles driven by total strangers to be extremely dangerous. It would perhaps have been more dangerous if we had been hurtling at the legal speed limit. We were, in fact, going somewhat slower than that because it was rush hour at the time. So, I prayed, as usual, that God would protect me from all those strangers and their vehicles.

It was Thursday evening, and I was relieved to be off work. I was also glad that I was on my way to Taekwon-Do class instead of going straight home, not that there was anything wrong with going straight home. My wife, son and daughter were a lot of fun and good company. They were all out of town for a few more days. She had a great opportunity for training paid for by her company, and she wanted to bring the kids along because they would be only a short distance from her mother's house in Seattle. The kids would stay with their grandmother, and their mother would attend meetings during the days. They would all have fun without me. That was okay. I had to work anyway.

But Taekwon-Do was fun too. We were all Black Tabs and helped our instructor teach class to the lower-ranked students. No, we were not Black Belts yet, but Black Tabs. That's what they call the Red Belts who have the black stripes, or tabs, on one end of their belts.

We had gone through all ten of the Gup levels, or the colored belt levels below Black, and we were all going to test for First Degree Black Belt next Saturday. Was it really only nine days away? It was hard to believe that finally the time had come to test for our Black Belts. How long *has* it been? Let's see

- now, it was over two years ago. It was in September; I remember school had started. The Labor Day holiday was just over, and my wife had plans to check out a new program for month-long free classes with someone at our church who was opening up a Taekwon-Do school. I figured she was getting our son and daughter into another athletic program, like karate for the kids. How long would that last? At first I didn't even realize that all four of us were going to try it.

The traffic was pretty usual as I drove. I wished, as usual, that we weren't going so slow. Oh, well, that just gave me more time to pray. I was the prayer leader in my Sunday school class at church. I wrote down prayer requests and prayed aloud for the class before we started our discussion of the Scriptures. The class was only about five or six couples around my age, and the requests never seemed especially dramatic. People seem to slow down and become content when they approach forty, or so it was with this group. If our class was ever visited by a couple that had something exciting or interesting to share with us, they seemed to never stay longer than a year. But the regulars, as friendly and nice as they were, were not very enthusiastic. We also had gone through about three different teachers in the four years I had attended that class.

But these days, or weeks, I had been praying a prayer along my commute. In addition to the need for God's protection in the dangerous traffic, I was also praying as the Bible instructs, without ceasing, about another thing. It was this: I sensed a great desire within me to get out of my usual job. No big deal, you might think. I had this great desire to become something else – something I really believed in, something you might call "a better purpose." I had been going to four different office jobs over the last fourteen years without complaint. I was fulfilling a great career and was very fortunate. But now something felt different. I had a prayer that wasn't just about me, but I think God wanted me to pray for a change. Does that make sense? Maybe you've felt the same way before. I hope so, because it's too hard to explain it any better than that.

So I repeated the prayer I had prayed every day for about five or six weeks, I guess. I reminded God that I wanted this change, and I explained again how it seemed best that I get a new way to make a living, leaving the details up to him. More money would be nice, but that didn't really seem appropriate for this particular prayer – I already made more money than a lot of people. But I wanted a better purpose, if you know what I mean. I don't know if the exact words were important. I didn't think so at the time because I figured God could read my thoughts anyway.

But this Thursday I sensed that God got the message. No, that isn't really right – it was I that got the message. It was a bit weird, and I actually thought at first that I must be just imagining things. But this time, well, it gave me a sort of peace, and I was ready to relax. I had never before felt that a prayer was suddenly answered and I could stop praying, but that is what happened. Right there in my vehicle on the highway going sixty-five miles per hour, something changed. It was as if I was ready for something new. Something good was about to happen. And suddenly, I saw a message from God, which gave me a surprise. It was a stop sign, affixed to the vehicle in front of me.

I believed that perhaps it was illegal to have a big red octagonal stop sign right on the tailgate of a truck traveling down the highway, but that is exactly what the truck in front of me had on it. Maybe you disagree, but I knew it was a sign from God and it was for me. He wanted me to quit praying that prayer and consider the matter done.

Yes, the traffic had sped up a little as we got farther away from the inner parts of the city. I was able to negotiate my exit from the highway without any usual commotion where the traffic lanes merged. I was now off the highway, but the traffic was no better. It was slower now, and there were more cars and trucks here trying to get into the right lanes of the multi-lane frontage road for their turns. I was no exception as I made my way across to the far-right lane slowly but surely.

Then, I was snapped to attention by the sound of squealing tires. I was able to smell the odor of hot brakes and burning rubber tires, and a semi-trailer truck stopped suddenly to avoid a collision. But I was not in the way of that trouble. It was ahead and to my left, but I needed to turn right at the second signal, so I was clear. But I was dazed by that heart-startling jerk that occurs when you hear unexpected traffic noises. I guess it's a form of mild shock, like when we witness dramatic or traumatic things. The traffic was as bad on the frontage road as it had been on the highway, but slower, so I pulled into a parking lot.

Once I had been paddling a canoe with a friend, and the white water capsized the boat. I remember being underwater with no possible way to move anywhere except where the water took me. If I had been smashed against a rock or thrown over a waterfall or held under the water until I drowned, I couldn't have done anything about it. That's how it felt to turn into that parking lot. I had passed by this parking lot a thousand times and never once entered it. A little while later I realized that I had not actually pulled into the parking lot, but someone else had done it for me. Yeah, I know that doesn't make sense, but that is exactly what happened. I actually moved the steering wheel and made the turn, but it was not by my will that it happened. Oh, I was still awake and quite aware of my surroundings. But this was just like watching yourself do something you had no intention of doing. I don't know why I didn't feel afraid that someone was trying to hurt me. Somehow this was all part of the answer to my prayer. I knew that, and it made it okay. Perhaps I should have felt violated because, after all, some force outside myself was causing me to go where I did not choose to go. Some rapid white water was taking me somewhere, and moving water is very powerful stuff. It has lots of momentum.

But there was no danger, and I was on the right side of God. So I watched with some fascination as I drove my Camry into the Nissan dealership parking lot. I wondered if a salesman would try to sell me a car when I stopped. That's how I felt - sort of goofy - like, Is this really happening, and why? But I, or someone, drove my car around to the back where there were other parking lots and other buildings. We were making our way...*We?*...to what looked like a parking garage. As I entered the garage, it seemed to make sense that there were no other people around, at least none that paid any attention to me. I was just another driver in another ordinary vehicle. The Camry is probably the most common car on the road around here, so what's to notice? Someone wanted me to be out of sight when something happened.

This actually did insert a bit of a fear factor into the equation when I thought about it, but there was no time to dwell on that. When my "something" happened, it was very fast, very sudden, quite painless, and very simple. The parking garage disappeared and some new walls appeared. And there I was blinking and sitting in my car in a nice living room somewhere.

Chapter 2 - Something Begins

The light was a bit brighter here than it had been in the parking garage. It seemed like indoor lighting for some reason. This living room turned out to be rather sparsely furnished. There was a small table with a vase of red flowers in front of me by the wall next to a curtained doorway. As I sat there trying to stay calm and keep a clear head, as they say, I realized that it wasn't really much of a living room at all. The reason I had thought of a living room was the flowers and the curtains. The curtains were a lot like the ones we have in our living room on the front windows, but these were simple and not lacy on the edges like ours. They were in a doorway, more like an archway, in the wall in front of me. The opening did not have a solid door in it but only the white curtains, which prevented me from seeing through. It was about as wide as two normal doors in my house, perhaps eight feet across and high. The curtains did not move with a breeze like they might have if the doorway led to the outside. I got the impression it was an interior doorway.

The wall with the flowers and the arched doorway with the curtains was what I saw first, because it was directly in front of me, and that wall had little else about it to describe. It seemed white, even though it wasn't, much like we are so used to in our own houses with the off-white painted walls. There was actually some fine texture to the wall surface, much finer and neater than the roughness we are so used to in the walls of my old house. This had a sort of natural look to me, like a smooth rock surface or the texture of a sandy beach, only solid. The wall went up to meet a ceiling but had rounded corners. I wasn't sure if I liked the effect, but that was because it was not normal to me. It probably was very normal here, I supposed. The ceiling height was not much different than any normal living room I've been in. But then I noticed the holes, or dots. Along the ceiling there were small openings about every five feet or so in the wall, round holes that were just too black to see what, if anything, was in them.

And as I turned to look at the rest of the view from my car, I saw that these holes went all around the room. It was a room about thirty feet wide and fifty feet long, with my car sitting in the exact middle of it. The two longer side walls had the same texture and color, but only one other feature. There was a line forming a rectangular shape of the same wall material about twenty feet wide and six or eight feet high in the wall to my left. I imagined that perhaps this rectangle could be opened like a window to allow someone to see out of the room. Perhaps it was a one-way window and someone was looking in at me now. It was not there for decoration because it was no different from the rest of the walls. Because it was so ordinary, I wondered why it was there. It looked like a repair job done up to deliberately not blend in very well.

The wall behind me also had a door in it. This too was arched like the opening in the front wall but had a solid door with no knob or hinges in it. It was a normal sized door like we have in our homes, only with arched corners. The shape was very nice, actually, because of the curves. The door was tightly shut.

As I sat there in the driver's seat and turned around to look at the door behind me, many thoughts were racing through my head. I was also trying to be alert, but there was no movement, not even a rustle of the curtain, and no sound beside the running of my car's engine for a long time, maybe three minutes. I laughed my little nasal "hmph," which my wife sometimes found irritating, when I realized the engine was running here in someone's living room. I didn't shut off the engine right away. I wanted to consider every detail about my situation, especially what danger I might be in, and I didn't want to miss anything. And I was trying to deliberately stay calm. Looking back on it now, I like to think it was my Taekwon-Do attitude of calm defense keeping me patient and, hopefully, ready for anything.

For some reason I thought there was carpet on the floor, but when I looked, it was actually grass. The indoor well-manicured lawn was the strangest thing I had seen so far, aside from the obvious fact that I was here at all. I wasn't sure what this grass carpet meant, but I was glad I had noticed, and it seemed to help me orient myself as a guest in someone else's living room, or whatever this room was. I think I had the feeling someone was going to start explaining things to me eventually and I didn't want too many surprises. The flowers looked like roses and were very nice.

I shut off the engine but left the keys in the dash. I usually never do this except when I am turning the car over to a mechanic for maintenance or to a valet parking attendant, and even then I often grab the keys and put them in my pocket out of habit. I began thinking of everything in my pockets and whether I would need my keys, my few coins, my wallet, my reading glasses, or my comb. Not only that, but was I dressed correctly for whatever I was about to experience? I was wearing the clothes I had worn to the office that day, which were slacks and a long-sleeved shirt with a tie. I wondered how long this was going to take. Was I ever going home? Was I going to live through this? I thought of my wife and kids and the Taekwon-Do class tonight. This is Thursday, nine days before my Black Belt test.

Oh, my God! What is happening? What can I do? What is this? Why?

Fear - the real thing - hit me like it had never hit me before. I was about to break down and scream, I thought, or cower to my knees if I could. I started shaking, and I wanted to cry. I wanted to make all this stop. I had to get a grip, remain calm. Could I do this, whatever it was going to be?

So I prayed.

As I looked at the keys hanging from the ignition switch, I was relieved to realize that I was no longer being controlled by the same force that had steered me and my car into that parking garage. I was doing only what I chose to do and thinking only what I chose to think without interference. Whoever was doing all this, whoever had brought me here, was now just waiting and leaving me alone. This thought gave me back some of my sanity, and my prayers gave me the one thing I needed most, to trust God, who loved me, and not to rely only on myself. After all, hadn't I decided when I became a believer that death was not something to fear, but that death would bring me to heaven and the presence of my Lord and Savior? So, I was comforted. Now what?

Something had to happen eventually. Why would anyone bring me here to sit and wait? Maybe the exhaust fumes from my car took them by surprise and they had to turn up the air conditioner. I supposed some scientific technology had transported me here or given me the impression that I had been transported here. I looked at my watch. It was still evening, with rush hour and sunset, and I wasn't expected at Taekwon-Do class for a while yet. Apparently I had only left that parking garage a few minutes ago.

Then the "action" suddenly began. Sorry, don't get excited yet; that's just a figure of speech. The action began very quietly and gently. I noticed it out of the corner of my eye, and I focused my attention there. Something had changed after five long minutes.

There was something written on the wall in the middle of that window-like rectangle on my left. I was sure the writing hadn't been there before. I supposed the wall may be acting as a projection screen or a sort of TV monitor. The words were in plain English in clear black lettering with proper sentence punctuation and capitalization. It said:

Please step out of your vehicle, and we will introduce ourselves to you.

That's all. I supposed they would now wait to see if I would obey the polite instruction.

I actually had considered that the air may not be fit to breathe from either my own car's exhaust fumes or for other more bizarre reasons I was reluctant to consider. But the fact that my car engine needed oxygen to run normally made me feel somewhat at ease about stepping out of the vehicle. And the fact that my car was not made to seal out the atmosphere around it and probably leaked like a sieve also made me trust the air in the surrounding living room. If there had been any poisons in the air or a lack of oxygen, I figured my car wouldn't have protected me this long anyhow, so I stepped out of the car and stood facing the writing on the wall.

The room actually felt almost too cool, but smelled nice, sort of like the outdoors. The grass floor was flat like a man-made floor, and the grass was very finely bladed and comfortable as a carpet. My shoes didn't allow me to actually feel it, and I wanted to bend down and touch it with my hand to see if it was real. But I remained standing and listening. I wanted to be ready for more action, now that I had obeyed the instructions on the big wall screen. Nevertheless, I remember that I distinctly believed it was real grass, because it smelled like a lawn. But someone must be watching me.

Nothing happened for another minute. The words remained on the screen, as if politely giving me enough time to read all of them thoroughly. But then I heard a voice to my right. I turned a bit too hastily to see a man step through the curtained archway. A woman followed him, and they took only a few steps into the room toward me before stopping beside each other, much like a married couple might stand to greet a guest in their living room.

However, I suppose I didn't act like a guest should act, as I was startled by their appearance. They wore decent outdoor summer clothing. They both wore shorts and a loose-fitting shirt. Her shirt was more of a blouse and feminine. I find it hard to explain now because their clothing was so normal that I hardly noticed it. Their clothes made them look male and female like normal people in my hometown, but these people were not from my hometown. They were not from Earth and not even human. They were green.

The color was actually a sort of blue-green but was not ugly or strange at all once you got over the initial surprise. Their hair was more human. His hair was black and her hair was brunette, which I thought contrasted strangely with her skin tone. But the shape and size of their bodies and limbs appeared to be human - five fingers on each hand and five toes on each sandaled foot. I wondered if perhaps these were humans with painted skin, and I had a thought that this whole thing was a practical joke and someone was trying to fool me with costumes and makeup. But then I noticed their skin was textured like the walls of the room and very rough, like leather, compared to human skin.

And there were other differences. The eyes were wrong. I couldn't figure out what was wrong with their eyes for a long time, but it was the irises. We say among our fellow beings on Earth that a person has blue eyes or brown or hazel eyes. But this man's eyes were yellow like a cat, and hers were of a blue I'd ever seen. The round irises were not flecked or streaked, but a solid bright color. And then I realized that the white part of the eye was not white, and I think this explains the eeriness more than any one thing. The whites of their eyes were light green, like lime sherbet, and the moisture of their tears seemed luminous. In spite of all these oddities, I thought I got used to it rather quickly.

They seemed to understand that I wanted to stare at them for a minute or two. But I felt awkward after I realized I was staring, and I think I made some incoherent amazed sounds, but I don't remember saying anything. They also looked at me as if to study my features but in a more polite way, as if they were not as surprised by my appearance as I was by theirs. That made sense, because they had just kidnapped me with some preconceived plan that must have involved a prior knowledge of my physiology, or so I assumed.

He spoke first. He simply said, "Hello, Mr. Adrien."

I replied, "Hello."

And then he said, "As far as we can tell, you are acting normal under these circumstances, and you have no need for assistance. However, if you need anything, please tell us."

He waited to see if I wished to respond, but I hadn't quite got my conversation tongue in gear yet. So, after the long pause, he continued, "We have studied your people for some time, but we may not be aware of all aspects of your physical and other needs. Please help us to make sure that you are comfortable and healthy. We do not wish to harm you in any way, and we apologize for any harm we may have done to you. Is there anything you need immediately?"

The last word was spoken, for some reason, as if it was an awkward afterthought. I tried to consider everything he said as I became aware of my own astonishment. I may have missed some of the things he said, being distracted by this whole crazy experience. But once I realized this was quite a normal conversation in English, I responded, "I'm fine. I just want to know who you are, where we are, and why I am here."

Then the woman spoke. "These are the questions we expected you to ask. Our answers can be told with a story. We will tell you the answer to your three questions and many other things if you will listen. The schedule has been made to allow for this. Would you like to hear the story now?"

Chapter 3 – The Story

Their voices were really quite normal, and they spoke English well. Surely it wasn't their native tongue if they were from another planet. However, there was a quality you would be advised to remember as you read this story that I cannot explain in writing very well. They often emphasized the words incorrectly and sometimes hesitated as if they were searching for the words. To a certain degree, of course, this would be expected of anyone who learned English as a second language. But there was another strangeness in their speech for some other reason. At the time it sounded like they had some trouble understanding the meaning of many of our English words but used them anyway.

I thought about the question she had asked me a little too long, but she did not prompt me to answer. They both just waited and calmly watched me. I was considering how to respond, whether I should be demanding and aggressive or whether I should submit and listen. I was taking in a bit much for an average earthling. I heaved a sigh as I realized that I really had no choice. They had demonstrated a power over me, which had so far remained friendly, but had a great potential for being unfriendly. The force that drove my car into that parking garage was quite compelling to remember. So, I said, "Yes, I would like to hear your story."

He began after a short pause. "My name is Mr. Temm. This is Ravsen, my wife. Our home was on a planet in the same galaxy as Earth. We are now in a vessel landed on the Earth's moon, having traveled here from our planet. We were not certain if your people could detect our presence here when we first arrived, so we have placed ourselves on the side of the moon not visible to earthlings."

Now the woman spoke again. "We came upon your planet in our travels and were quite surprised to find such a population there. All the planets we have visited prior to yours were either populated with only animals and birds, with only plant life, or were entirely void of life. Most were incapable of sustaining any kind of life at all. When we realized the extent of your world's population, we remained here to observe and learn from you."

Both Mr. Temm and Ravsen remained quiet for a moment after this, so I took the opportunity to interject with my human nature. "Could we sit down or something? Is this going to be a long story? Perhaps we could have some refreshment of some kind? I don't mind waiting a while to eat, but some water would be nice." I remembered that they had asked me if I needed anything, but when I considered it, I really wasn't able to think about food. I was used to waiting until after Taekwon-Do class to eat, and that was often rather late. Here, with these interesting aliens, I was actually stalling for time. Things were going a bit too fast for me, and I needed something to help me regain some control.

They looked at each other but still seemed calm and friendly. Without speaking, Mr. Temm lifted his right hand and made a small waving gesture in no particular direction. As I looked around casually, I noticed the writing had gone from the wall. Soon after they resumed their story a second man came into the room with a sort of pitcher. It looked like it was made of a plant husk but was nicely shaped. Mr. Temm drank out of it and passed it to me. He and his wife watched quietly as I took a sip. It was indeed water, plain and cool, not cold and not iced. I tried to be polite as I offered the pitcher to Ravsen. She accepted it and also drank, as if all this was completely normal and ordinary behavior, which it was, right?

When the man with the pitcher left, another man and a woman came in. They looked younger than Mr. Temm and Ravsen, and they had chairs for us to sit in. There were only two chairs, and they were deliberately set behind Ravsen and me, leaving Mr. Temm without one. I sat down only after Ravsen sat first. No chair was ever brought for Mr. Temm, nor did the matter enter the conversation. Okay, sitting in chairs was nothing to talk about here - I was catching on. The chairs seemed to be made of ordinary wood and were not especially comfortable, anyway.

Mr. Temm continued the story. "My words so far have answered your questions about who we are and where we are now located, at least in a simple way. The portion of the story that will answer your question as to why we have brought you here will involve more time. It may at first seem that I am not speaking to the subject, so I ask in advance that you listen patiently as I explain, as quickly as I can, why we have brought you here."

He spoke these words with that strange quality I referred to earlier. He spoke with such urgency that I was apparently visibly surprised because he continued with some satisfaction, as if he had made a great point. So, he wanted me to listen carefully and pay attention. I felt like a child being scolded, yet he reverted back to his polite speech quickly enough. "We have read of the origins of your people on Earth, and we have seen the results of that origin in the people who now live on your planet. Our planet had similar origins, but a different outcome."

He remained silent a bit too long for my taste, but Ravsen took up the story eventually. "We may not have made it clear to you how...different your people are to us and how we were...shocked and confused by your civilization. It was very difficult, for example, for us to learn your language because the words and ideas are foreign to us. We do not have things like hatred, violence, warfare, weapons. We do not have concrete roadways and steel weather stations in the sky. We do not understand the need to rush or hurry. We do not have impatience in our world, nor do we have treachery, sophistry, and so many other things strange and odd to us. There is a great difference in us which has made us learn to struggle with our own..."

She stopped and remained silent, and for some time both of them seemed to be thinking about some inner personal things. I went ahead and said, "I understand."

They looked at me with great surprise, just as a human would, with wide eyes and parted lips. They seemed to want me to explain myself, so I tried something. "My people have always known we were bad. We make laws to protect ourselves from each other. We make borders and fences to keep enemies away. We build machines to make us powerful so we can control others, all in the name of self-protection. I suppose if your world managed to avoid warfare and stayed peaceful, it would certainly be confusing to see how we treat each other here."

Mr. Temm resumed his speaking with this chance to divert the story in a more practical direction. They had been, for some reason, distracted from telling their story, lost in thought. It was actually the rudest thing they had done to me so far, aside from kidnapping me. I'm not complaining because they were nice enough. I was just glad my abductors weren't raving lunatics bent on destruction and death. These greenish, nice people were a much better sort than many Earth people.

"Yes, but the difference between your people and ours is much deeper. We believe we have found the specific detail that makes us so different, and this discovery has opened our eyes to something we regret somewhat to have seen. In fact, many of us are of an opinion that we cannot return to our home planet, now that we have seen yours. It would bring the same regret to the people there if we told our story."

At these words, along with his way of saying them, I started to understand that these people were feeling some sort of disgust or loathing for the cruel and self-centered normal behavior of my fellow race on Earth. They were repulsed, even sickened, by the lifestyle my people had gotten used to over the course of history. I found this a rather extreme reaction, and I asked Mr. Temm with visible passion perhaps, "Surely you can't mean that simply seeing and watching our people, our planet, has made you dirty or something, can you? Are you suggesting that we are so bad that whoever comes in contact with us turns bad too?"

In my mind I was wondering if this might indeed be a true reflection of my human race, but I couldn't bring myself to cheerfully agree to such a thing.

Mr. Temm seemed to be trying to think of what to say or perhaps he was not sure if he understood what I had said, so Ravsen spoke instead. "What you are saying is perhaps true in a certain way, we do not know. The truth is so much of your world is unknown to our entire experience, we have had a difficult time coordinating and processing all of the information. In our world, there has been only a very few deaths, and our Lord God has assured us that those few who have died have been removed from us only temporarily and that we will be reunited with them at the end of the ages. The tale of the first shedding of blood is a favorite among us, but most of our people have never seen blood. Though there have been very few deaths on our planet, most of them are from the drowning of those who failed in their attempt to cross the sea. Consider then, if you can, what it may be like to us to see the blood spilled daily on your planet and the deaths of so many celebrated with funerals every day."

I wasn't sure if had she used the word "celebrated" correctly, but I got her point. "Yes, I suppose that is a horrible sight. But I am not sure if I understood you correctly on one point. Perhaps your use of my language, as fluent as it is, has left me confused. If you say that there are very few deaths on your planet, I suppose you mean there are very few murders or accidental deaths among the younger people. Surely the natural course of death from old age has brought many deaths to the people throughout the history of your planet. Do you not also have funerals for those who die quietly in their beds?"

Ravsen did not speak immediately, but that was her usual habit, so I waited. But Mr. Temm spoke next. "The specific detail that makes our peoples so different, which I spoke of before, is the fact that your Adam and Eve disobeyed God's command, but our father and mother did not. Your Adam and Eve were cursed with death, but our father and mother were not. People do not die on our planet." He stopped here and acted as though that was a good place to end the conversation. However, seeing my apparently incredulous expression, he added a few more words. "The people on our home planet have not died of old age or for any other reason, except those few Ravsen told you about, since the day the first man was created. That man is still alive after over ten thousand years. He is my grandfather.

Chapter 4 - The Need

Their voices were silent for a while as I pondered this. No death. No sin. A world like the Garden of Eden for thousands of years. Adam and Eve, before the great Fall, were naked and unashamed. They walked with God in the cool of the day. What if Eve had answered back to the Serpent and decided instead to obey God. I imagine she could have said, "Excuse me, Serpent, while I go and fetch my husband so we can both together consider your fruit offer." Or better yet, what if she and Adam called on God, who was always there for them, and asked his advice before answering the Serpent?

I asked Mr. Temm and Ravsen, "Were your mother and father tempted by an evil one to disobey, like Adam and Eve?"

"Yes, they were. But they asked God to give them reminders of the correct way. Their reply was 'No' to the Evil One. Our stories tell us that the Evil One left and was greatly diminished thereafter, but it is said that he caused the few deaths that have occurred in our world since."

His wife said, "We see that the Evil One is not so diminished after all in your world, and other worlds that we know - one other, at least."

We stopped speaking for a while. We were all considering our own thoughts, I suppose. Who knows how much these people might suffer if they watched my miserable planet much longer. I wondered if there was anything good that could come out of this.

I had very little pride in my own people that Thursday evening on the back side of the moon. I looked at my watch. It was time for me to be in Taekwon-Do class. I supposed there was nobody who was going to worry about me. After all, I showed up to class at different times, depending on the day of the week, and sometimes I had to work late at the office. And I wasn't expected to be there every time the doors were open. My family was not expected back until Wednesday. Perhaps they would find my car in that parking garage and there would be an investigation. No, I had forgotten. My car was *here*. I looked over my shoulder, and there it was, a bit dirty, with a few dents and scratches - same old car.

"Why did you bring me here?"

Mr. Temm looked down at me, and I saw what looked like a man who should have wanted to cry but did not know how because no one had ever taught him. "We need you."

Ravsen didn't wait as long as usual, but spoke up right then. "There are forty-eight of us on this vessel. We have all seen the new things in your world. We all feel haunted and tainted by what we have seen and heard. There was no hope, and many of us agreed that it would be impossible to return home to our family. But we asked the Lord our God to provide us with some hope, and he has done so. There is a new detail that will allow us to make some atonement for the things we have come to know from watching your world. There is a way we can be cleaned and freed from our haunting.

"We saw a creature, perhaps the Evil One himself, come to this planet system. He is now landed on the satellite Dione, which orbits the planet Saturn. He has a weapon we believe he has used on other planets before. We have seen evidence of it on some of those we visited and did not know what to think of it at the time. But now we believe this creature is planning to use his weapon on your Earth."

She sat looking at me with a great smile, as if I should be pleased by this information. On the contrary, I was stunned and not pleased at all. "That's horrible!" I stood up from my chair. "There must be something you can do! We've got to warn them! Can you destroy this creature before he fires his weapon?"

Mr. Temm spoke with a calm and simple voice, "No, but you can."

"What do you mean, *no*? And what do you mean, *I* can?"

"I mean we cannot because we have never destroyed anything in our lives, and we are not able to begin doing so now for risk of great consequence akin to Adam and Eve's punishment. We are thankful that if we were to disobey our Lord God, and may it never be so, we are far enough away from our planet that those who remain there would never be affected by the consequences of our actions. Remember, Mr. Adrien, we have not known the word "kill" until we learned your language. Perhaps our knowing that one word is enough to condemn our entire planet, should we return there and utter it once. We do not know. We must be stronger than ever, now that we have such knowledge to bear. The Lord our God is with us.

"I also mean for you to understand that the reason we brought you here is so that we can gain our freedom by enabling you to save your planet from destruction. If you are willing to do this act, then we, through aiding you, will have been responsible for doing a good deed."

His great, big green smile was sickening to me, but I understood. He was innocent, naïve, and ignorant of so much. He must think of me, of all earthlings, as assassins and murderers. Why did this conversation have to be so negative and down, all about the sin and wickedness of my human race?

But maybe there was something of value going on here after all. I ventured to play along, to see where this was going to go, but I was feeling a bit sick in my gut and not sure if I could continue this whole dream. Nightmare. At that exact moment, I had no intention of trying to spar with some sort of alien creature on Saturn and likely die in the process. But there was more to come. Wait till you hear the next part.

"Your vehicle can easily be equipped for space travel, and we can just as easily teach you how to fly it." Ravsen was telling me some of the details about the mission I was being offered, like I had a choice. If there really was an evil creature on Saturn's moon, and if he really intended to aim a weapon at Earth, then I either had to figure out how to stop it or I had to leave forever with these green aliens and let my whole home world get blown to bits. I was tempted to do just that, but I knew I had to listen to these people, and I knew I had to try my best to help.

It was amazing to me that Mr. Temm and his people did not really seem to care about saving Earth so much as in regaining their own honor. But, I had to remember, they never had to save anyone from anything on their garden planet, except maybe save a child from a falling rock. But an act like that would not be noble or valuable, I suppose. Who am I kidding, there was no such thing as noble or valuable acts on their planet. They had never needed them.

On their planet, for thousands of years, there had been no diseases, medicine, or any need of any kind. These few folks here were likely wearing clothes only for my benefit. At home they probably never even thought of clothing themselves. Why would they? They really didn't need tools very much until someone had the idea that they would like to cross the sea to see what was on the other side. This led to boats, ships, and eventually airplanes. The pattern is obvious, and the trend eventually led them to the stars.

But their technology was stupendous. The best I could figure it, they understood the inner workings of everything down to the subatomic levels, and they could manipulate matter with energy in any form. They could do this because of a pure relationship with God, who had created it all.

But many of the people did not care about travel. There was no need to hurry because no one ever died. It is amazing how we earthlings are always in such a hurry because we know we have to die someday. You don't have to agree with me because it's just a theory. Anyway, there were only the forty-eight people who really wanted to go once the ship was ready. I wondered how long they've been traveling around the galaxy. Mr. Temm never seemed to comprehend my questions about time or how long things take. He just shrugged as if he didn't have the time to learn the way our clocks and calendars work along with everything else he had already had to learn.

I didn't have a lot of time for theorizing and chitchatting with my new friends. The schedule had been made. Yes, even though these people seemed to have no concern for the passing of time, they knew down to the minute how long it would take for that evil creature's weapon to become functional. I had no idea how they could monitor something or someone on a distant planet, but they knew all about this creature. Actually, Mr. Temm did not know where the creature was from, nor if there were others like him, but he knew everything you can know about someone from watching, listening, and measuring. My green friends had not tried to communicate with the bad creature, and as far as they knew, the creature didn't know we existed here on the Earth's moon. Or if he did, he didn't think we were worth his attention.

After our conversation on my first evening with Mr. Temm and Ravsen, I got to eat some food. Too bad there is nothing to tell about the food. It seems they were able to get or make food exactly like we have on Earth. I just had to tell them what I wanted, and they served it up in a short while. I was almost embarrassed while we were discussing food. I felt like a patron in a restaurant for which I wasn't adequately dressed. I usually don't order beer with my meals, except when the kids aren't around. That was the best bottle of Guinness I ever had, I must admit. They must have got it from Dublin. But they did not eat with me. I sat at a table with a red rose, and everything was too quiet. We didn't really interact very much again before they insisted that I sleep. They took me through the door in the wall behind the Camry and down a hall to a sort of bedroom. It had very simple furnishings, sort of like the Garden of Eden might have, I suppose. I assumed my flight training would proceed when I awoke, but this training was not what I expected.

Chapter 5 – The Belt Tabs

I was under the impression that something suspicious had happened while I was sleeping, for some reason. It was as if something had been done to me, but I couldn't figure what that might be. At first, I supposed that they had induced my sleep, like in the movies when they slip a drug into the hero's coffee while his back is turned, and he wakes up a few hours later, locked up as a prisoner.

But when I woke up, I was not locked in. I went back to the room where my car was. I had tried halfheartedly to wander around looking through the ship while I was still barefoot in the early morning. That was when I realized the grass used as a carpet in some of the rooms was real and very soft. Other floors were textured with the same grain as the walls, and some were very smooth and hard. I could not discern any pattern for the differences, however. It was also interesting to discover that the floors were warm.

But it turned out there were no doors or passages to wander through. Everything was either locked or simply a dead-end wall. The area where I was had only a simple hall with a few doors. After I got dressed back in my room into the same clothes I had been wearing the day before, I went back to where I assumed I should report. I had no choice, really.

The door back into the room where my car was had been shut, but it opened when I touched it. There was something high-tech about the way it worked, but I didn't understand it. It opened like it was electrically powered, but it could have been just a nice, smooth, mechanically balanced system with hinges on ball bearings or something, maybe with some counterweights hidden in the walls. I was a civil engineer, specialized in steel and concrete structures, but I had some appreciation for the smaller contrivances of the mechanical engineers too. These door hinges were very nice and quite amazing in their quality.

I found my car. There were two people with it: one was Mr. Temm, and the other was a man wearing basic human clothes like the others had worn. The other man smiled at me but said nothing. By now I knew that these people were going out of their way to be accommodating and friendly to me. I was apparently a sort of celebrity to these forty-eight space travelers. They had chosen me to help them atone for their problem emotions and troubles. I wanted to find out why they chose me out of all the possible choices that must have existed. I was going to try to find out if I got a chance.

I spoke to them as I entered. "Good morning, Mr. Temm." I immediately realized that it was questionable whether this was indeed morning under these circumstances, but he responded easily enough. My watch told me that it was early Friday morning, so I had slept a healthy eight hours. At that time, I did not think about the fact that I should have called into the office or that I was already later than usual getting there. The truth is, I would never be reporting back to the office at all. Looking back, I think I was actually somewhat excited about the prospect these aliens represented to me, and my life in that engineering office on Earth had already taken a back seat.

"Good morning, Mr. Adrien." I half expected him to introduce the other man who was working on something under the hood of my car, but it did not surprise me when he remained silent. Introducing a companion to a stranger was not part of their habitual ways. Mr. Temm spoke to the other man before looking back at me. And, believe it or not, he spoke in a foreign language. I know I should not have been surprised. I had no reason to think that the entire crew of this ship had learned English. Perhaps only Mr. Temm and Ravsen had the ability to talk with me.

Mr. Temm turned back to me with a smile. "There is breakfast if you wish to eat." He waved to the small table in the corner of the room near the curtained doorway. The red rose was gone now, replaced by something resembling a daisy. There was now a bowl of fruit there too. He watched as I took an apple. As I bit into it, he became businesslike. "We have almost completed the equipping of your vehicle for use as a spacecraft. Your training will occur when you are ready, and everything you will need to know to operate your vehicle with our added features will be included. The schedule allows you to wait about three hours from now before we must insist that you begin the training. Is this a sufficient amount of time for you?"

This was a little odd because I had never actually agreed to go on this mission. I understood they were offering me this opportunity, or requesting my help, but, well, now it looked like the mission was being planned before I had said anything about it. So, I thought I would risk a little trouble. I spoke a bit loudly, "Maybe three hours is not enough. I haven't decided if I want to accept your proposal yet. I have some questions I want you to answer."

Mr. Temm stopped and turned toward me. He had not been expecting me to resist him this morning, but at that moment, he looked like he was about to pull a weapon out of a holster. Maybe I was a bit suspicious, but that's the way I saw it at the time. I tried to look confident, even though I wasn't, as he prepared to speak to me. *Here it comes*, I thought to myself. I tried to smile as he addressed me. "The training should answer all remaining questions. Mr. Adrien, the training will not be any danger to you. The entire mission will be no danger to you. Everything you need will be given to you. After you have destroyed the evil creature threatening your planet, you will be free to go."

He waited a moment to see if I had anything to say in response, but when I said nothing, he continued. "We are planning to give you...something of...value. We do not truly understand the concept of giving gifts, but many of us believe that we should prepare to offer you a reward or a payment for your services. We have seen the practice among the people of your planet, and we hoped that you would understand and that it would be good to you. Others of our group were afraid that you would be offended by an offer of payment.

"Would you like to have a reward for doing this mission? We will give you anything you wish, but perhaps we cannot do so unless you tell us what you wish. I apologize for our ignorance. We mean to act correctly. Your co-operation is valuable to us. Please tell me what we need to say or do to persuade you to help us." What had started out as anger in his voice and expression had changed and was now much softer. He seemed rather sensitive now, almost like he needed a friend and wanted me to like him.

This talk about a reward was starting to sound interesting, however. I had not given much thought to the idea of being "free to go" after all this was over. Could I really go back to my wife and kids and to my friends and family and resume where I left off? I wondered if I was going to get back in time for my Taekwon-Do test next Saturday. No, it looked like that might turn out to be impossible. How long could this training take? It must be days of information, or at least many hours. How long would it take to go to Saturn and back? My astronomy was a bit rusty, but I had learned that Saturn was something like two or three times farther from the Sun than the Earth.

No, I was dreaming if I thought my life was going to be normal again any time soon. But surely I would get home eventually, wouldn't I? I brought my thoughts back to Mr. Temm, who was patiently waiting for me to respond. Perhaps I could fix it so there were some improvements waiting for me when I did get home. "Did you say, 'anything I wish?'"

"Yes. Whatever you would like for us to give you is yours for the asking."

"Could you, for example, arrange for money in my bank account on Earth?"

"Yes. How much would you like?"

Things were now spinning through my head. This was a gold mine, if it were true. Could these people really do what Mr. Temm was suggesting? Could I save the planet and get rich at the same time? He said there would be no danger. How could that be? Everything seemed too good to be true. There must be a catch.

I forgot to ask him why it was me in particular that they had chosen for this mission. I was a bit distracted by the dollar signs floating past my eyes.

Well, I don't think I am a greedy person. I don't think I ever was. So I tried to consider what would be the right thing to do. I tried to draw up the feelings in my heart and do the right thing. I wanted some of that gold mine, but I didn't want to be a jerk. For the first time, I wanted to really help these people. As I stood there with an apple in my hand, looking at this green man in shorts and a leisure shirt, I felt sorry for him, all his people, his whole world. I really wanted to make a difference for them to take home, and I wanted them to be able to go home and rejoice with their families. I did not want to cause some sort of curse. I had a strange sensation, a great mixture of sadness and thankfulness. I felt like Adam and Eve were my own father and mother, and I respected them both. Somehow their sin had given God something to work with, something I could be thankful for, something we would never have had otherwise. I did not want to be like these green people. I needed my fear and hatred. I needed my violence and power. I needed my fences and my boundaries.

These people from another planet did not have sin, disease, or even death. But they also didn't know what a gift was. They didn't understand heroism, justice, mercy, or so many other things, things that I liked. So, here's what I said: "You are very generous. I must try to help you understand something, if I can. I want your gift or reward to be valuable. I want for you to figure out what to give me without me telling you what I want. I want you to take all the data you have about my people and assume that I will like whatever gift you give me without my picking it out for myself. It will make your gift more meaningful if you believe the value of the gift matches the value of the service I perform. So I will not tell you what I wish for you to give me. I will instead give you the freedom to chose for me what you wish me to have."

I had a sort of inspiration, and I continued, "Let me tell you a story of my own. Surely you have seen the various forms of martial arts found all over the world. They are in the movies, in books, and there are schools that teach all the various forms to the students who pay for them. People use martial arts for health training, self-defense, physical therapy, and fun, among other things.

"Well, in my Taekwon-Do school, when the students learn new material, which consists of various drills and patterns and techniques for various physical abilities, they earn belts of different colors to wear with their uniforms. And sometimes, instead of a new colored belt, they earn only a couple of strips of colored tape added to the end of their old belt. Consider the value of these strips of tape. This tape is worthless by itself and can be bought for a low price by the roll at any store. But when a student spends his time, his sweat, and his money to train in Taekwon-Do, there is a great event we call a test, where he performs his learned material before an audience. And in honor of his promotion to a higher rank, he receives his two pieces of colored tape. And I tell you, those two pieces of colored tape, placed upon his belt by his instructor in a sort of ceremony, are worth far more to him than many gifts that a lot of money could buy. The tape is valuable because it was earned, because it cost something dear to obtain it. The tape, which was a cheap item, becomes valuable because of its meaning. It is a medal of honor and achievement, and whether it is made of gold or of plastic makes no difference - he has *earned* it."

Well, I may have blown my chances to get rich, but it was definitely more right than naming a dollar figure for my heroic services. But I was not so pure and holy as I may have sounded. I had some plans to ask for more and perhaps to teach Mr. Temm a thing or two about monetary value in case he needed a refresher course. I also believed that this man had every intention of giving me a large reward. He was dead serious about it. They would give me whatever I asked them for. But I assumed then that there would be time for me to think about it before I made any specific requests. Certainly there would be plenty of time to ask for more.

I watched the expression on Mr. Temm's face, and he seemed to be truly interested in what I was saying. However, he did not say anything more. I hoped I had not confused matters or complicated the situation. He turned and spoke to the other man, who had finished with my car and shut the hood. I had not seen whether the engine under the hood of the Camry was any different now after the new accessories, whatever they were, had been installed, but I noticed that the hood did not slam the way it used to. Now it shut quietly with a sort of nice, soft hissing sound. But Mr. Temm's short discussion with his fellow crew member did not seem to be about our previous conversation. Perhaps they were simply talking about the business of equipping my car. After that, the other man left with a polite smile to me.

When we were alone again, Mr. Temm said, "I hope you will begin the training within the hour so our hope may continue."

I immediately answered, "Let's begin now, if you're ready."

This brought a new smile to Mr. Temm's green face. "Follow me."

Chapter 6 – The Training

If there had been anything special about the room, it had been those curtains. We were about to walk through them. It somehow felt like this was the part where I was about to enter into the mysterious space aliens' ship, so I hesitated a moment after my first step toward that curtained archway. Something was about to begin, and I felt like I needed to say good-bye to some part of my past. I wondered again if I could believe that I was not going to be in any danger. Mr. Temm had said so with great confidence, but everything he knew about danger he had learned from watching my planet. He probably didn't have a word for "danger" in his own language. I wondered how long they had been studying Earth. Did they really have a thorough and complete idea of what we were all about? How can anyone learn everything there is to know, read every book in every library in every country on Earth? Well, they seemed to know what they were doing; they had power, and I had no choice. Did I?

Mr. Temm stopped when he saw that I had stopped. I looked back at my car behind us, still in the center of the room where I had left it. It was clean now, but the dent on the driver's door was still there. It looked like some of the scratches were still there, but also clean and repainted the same blue color it had always been. Usually when a car gets painted the blemishes are also smoothed out, but these were still there. Oh, it wasn't bad. The car had never been in a wreck. It just seemed strange to see a car all clean and freshly painted, but with a few dings and dents. Oh, well, I wasn't going to explain to Mr. Temm that he did a bad job on my car. He obviously meant well, and besides, the work they had done was supposed to make my car fly and run properly, not look good.

I said to Mr. Temm when he looked at me with questioning eyes, "How long is this going to take?"

I really didn't need to ask this question. I suppose I was just stalling as I dealt with my feelings of loss. I was not as ready as I thought I had been to start this whole thing off and perhaps never return or be the same. I think I knew somehow that the word "training" meant something different here than what I had known before. "The duration of the training is variable, depending on your needs, your abilities, and your cooperation. As much as we know about you, we cannot know everything. We must see how well you train." I assumed he meant, "how well you learn," but I was not in the habit of correcting his grammar. I motioned for him to go ahead and lead the way again.

He pushed aside the curtain and stepped through the archway, and I followed. We went down hallways, through doors, around smooth corners at some odd angles and some not so odd. We went down an elevator. Some passages were wide; some were narrow. The shapes and sizes varied far more than they would in any vessel or building on Earth. There was really nothing about the place that was "architecture," as far as I was concerned.

Eventually we passed by a vast cavernous area too big to see in its entirety. We were on a sort of open catwalk elevated over the emptiness below us. My fear of heights kicked in a couple of times when the railing disappeared for a stretch or two, but I kept my cool and said nothing. I got the idea this must be a very large ship. The space contained what I assumed to be machinery and such, housed in boxlike containers, the way we might house our own engines and machines.

There was ductwork of all sizes, shapes, and diameters strewn over the ship, which looked disorganized to my eyes. Everywhere were earth-toned colors, greens and browns and tans. The texture varied some but not much or enough. It was all too much like the walls in the room that housed my car.

I noticed that there was not much sound. What I did hear was mostly conversation and the rustlings of people, because we did see other green-colored people. This ship was far too spacious for only forty-eight people, I thought, but then again, I didn't know what made this thing run or how much space they needed. The people were friendly to Mr. Temm and always looked at me just as you would look at the guest you knew was around here somewhere but you had not met yet. But all the conversation was in Mr. Temm's language, not English.

We arrived at our destination. It was a sort of laboratory room. There were machines and vessels, switches, tables, chairs, and shelves all over the place. Everything was nicely rounded and not like the sharp, crisp, shiny lab furniture we had on Earth. I didn't see any glass or metal, but there were small, delicate things and large, bulky things. There were doors to other chambers, unknown to me, and there were windows and doorways in that same random manner throughout the room. For as large an area as this was, there were few people here. Only three were within my field of vision as we entered, but I supposed there could be others nearby. I don't know if they wore clothing because I was here, or if they wore it because they wanted to. But all of their clothing looked like the stuff we wore on Earth. I assumed they got it from our planet. Those in the lab did not wear aprons or cloaks over their casual things like I expected lab technicians to wear. I guess there was nothing to spill here. Perhaps there was nothing toxic in their world at all.

Mr. Temm stopped and turned to me when we arrived in the middle of the room. The other three also turned to listen. I wondered if they could understand English. "You must enter into a chamber by yourself, Demetrius. Though you will be apart from us, we will still be able to hear you. However, you will not need to speak unless we ask you to. Your experience will be simply waiting. We must first take readings, and then the training can be prepared and implemented. You will then be able to pilot your Toyota Camry to Saturn to accomplish the mission. Please enter this chamber, and I will continue to explain, if you wish."

A woman with orange- and brown-striped hair waved me toward a door that opened by sliding sideways into the wall rather than swinging on hinges. She reminded me of our cat for some reason. I said, "Thank you," as I passed her. She spoke English with a weird accent and said, "Yerr welcome."

I stood in the small room and was disappointed that there was no chair. There was, in fact, nothing in the room. It was just a smaller version of any other room, but there were those small black holes spaced evenly in the walls near the ceiling just like in the room where all this began. These holes were more closely spaced, so there were more of them. The rounded corners seemed to distort my perspective, so I was a little bit disoriented. And there were no shadows either. My brain wanted there to be shadows and straight lines, but there weren't any.

I haven't mentioned the way everything was illuminated because I hadn't noticed it myself until then. All the lighting usually came from the ceiling. The whole ship just seemed to be lit up as needed without one knowing where the lights originated. I don't remember seeing any actual light sources on my entire walk through the ship. This room was no different. But now I looked at the ceiling and saw that it glowed. It was very nice natural lighting. The ceiling had the same rough texture as the other wall surfaces, as far as I could tell, but was brighter in the center of the room and difficult to focus on. I did not feel any heat as one might get from a light bulb or from the sun through a skylight.

Mr. Temm's voice resumed once I stopped and turned in the center of the room, looking back at the door as it shut. "Do you wish for me to continue to explain what is happening?"

"Yes. Please do." I did not intend to just wait for some surprise without an explanation. Some of the fear I had thought I was beyond tried to creep back in as Mr. Temm's voice resumed his explanation. I had to remind myself that these were friendly people who needed my help. They were not going to hurt me. That is what he had told me. I tried to listen.

"Once the readings are taken, which will give us all the additional data required to suit the training to your specific physiological settings, we will begin the process. If you wish, I will tell you when the training is about to begin. Do you wish for me to do so?"

"Yes."

"Very well. The training will consist of two separate phases. One is for your brain, where we will place the information you will need to operate your vehicle and to navigate the spaces in this vicinity of the galaxy. We have prepared a training program that will give you any data you may need for any conceivable or unlikely eventualities that may occur along the course of the mission. Please keep in mind that much of this data will not be needed, as all possibilities will certainly not occur during the mission. We simply need to make sure that if you should need to know something, the data will be there for you.

"The second phase is for the remainder of your body, which will need some repair work and new features. We need for you to be able to operate not only the controls for piloting your vehicle, but the weapons system, the emergency safety system, and all other systems that now are part of your vehicle."

I interjected a question here because I wasn't sure if I had heard him right. "What do you mean by 'repair work'?"

"There are a number of areas in your body with improperly functioning elements or inefficient processes. There is some evidence of deterioration in many of the bones, sinews, ligaments, muscles, and systems of your body. We believe this is a result of the aging process your people have endured, but we can do much to limit this in you while we have you here. If there is also some scar tissue, deformity, inadequate chemical processes, and other problems, then we can eliminate or diminish these for your ease of operation. As an added precaution, we will also take the liberty of increasing your abilities to see, hear, smell, taste, and touch, and we will improve many of the hindrances to efficiency that have resulted from your eating and breathing the foods and pollutants of your world. This is our endeavor to lessen the chance of any failure on your part to operate the equipment for lack of efficiency rather than lack of resources. You will find that you will have less need to sleep and you will find that from now on, the food and drink you consume will be more effectively digested.

"Mr. Adrien, I believe I have understood the story you told me yesterday, to a certain degree, and I have begun to give you a gift that will be worthy of the services you will perform for us. I am still considering the matter, and I am deciding what more to give you when you return from Saturn. Let these repairs be the beginning of a gift. I believe you will like the results."

I said nothing as I thought about this. I hoped they weren't going to operate on me. Perhaps they didn't consider that all these repairs might cause excruciating pain. Mr. Temm's voice seemed to echo as it said, "We are ready to begin the training." And then the light went out. I was in complete darkness, but I had no time to do anything about it. I fell asleep. Yes, you read me correctly; I don't think I have ever gone from wakefulness to complete sleep so abruptly before. All I knew was that I woke up standing exactly where I had been, in that same small chamber. The light was on again. I looked at my watch. It was still morning on Friday. I had been standing there asleep only a short time. Surely the training hadn't started yet.

Mr. Temm's voice spoke again, as if there had been no changes. "How do you feel, Mr. Adrien?"

"Fine. I feel fine." And I realized that I felt more than fine. I had felt good many times in my life before, like right after a vigorous workout or when some burden is lifted or when I heard good news. But this beat all of those times. I was healthy. I was now ready, alert, and collected like I had never been before. I wondered how long this was going to last and did I have time to do everything I needed to do while it lasted?

"Are there any ill effects we may have overlooked?" Great, this was a fine time to mention that there was a possibility they may have overlooked something. There had been no pain, no discomfort. I was glad they had not hurt me or operated on me in any surprising way while I was under their power.

I sensed that I was not under their power anymore. I knew everything I needed to know to do this mission and go home. They were not going to hurt me. My fear was gone, and my suspicion was unnecessary. These were truly innocent people who just wanted me to help them. I felt free.

"No, the training seems to have been very effective." I was aware that I now knew how to pilot a spacecraft - my spacecraft. I was aware that I now knew exactly how far away Saturn was at this time. And I knew some other things that vaguely surprised me, as I maintained a conversation with Mr. Temm. "How is your wife?"

The door opened, and there was Mr. Temm, smiling broadly. "She wants to name the baby Demetrius," he said.

I was stunned. "Wow. I am honored. Where did she learn so much about gift-giving? Please tell her I am greatly honored." I felt like my relationship with Mr. Temm had improved. I could trust him, and I understood him.

"I will. If you wish, we can begin your flight immediately. But we have some hours to spare, if you need time for anything."

"No, I think I should begin as soon as possible."

"Good. You know the way to your vehicle. We have moved it to the outer docking bay. Good luck!"

I knew that "good luck" was an expression he probably didn't understand. Hey, I wasn't sure I understood it myself anymore, but his eyes had a good joy in them. He and his people were soon to get their haunting lifted if I could destroy this creature on Dione and return here to report the mission accomplished. Oh, they would know whether I accomplished the mission long before I returned, but I needed to report back, if nothing else, just to say good-bye. And besides, the return trip to the moon was part of the schedule. I had not forgotten that Mr. Temm wanted to give me a gift when I returned.

Chapter 7 – The Mission

I went to the outer docking bay quickly, but I didn't run, because there was no real hurry. The schedule had already been made with all things considered. The evil creature's weapon would not be ready until a particular time. I knew what kind of weapon it was, even though no one on Earth had ever imagined one like it. I knew how it worked and what this creature was likely using it for.

As repulsive as it may seem, this creature fed on people. Yes, he ate them after they died and rotted for a couple of days. The evidence showed that he was a rogue, possibly banished by his own people. He and his people were as much like lizards as I was like a monkey. It was rather disturbing to think that it was probably an insult to this creature to call him a lizard. The weapon he was assembling was not from his world, but he must have found it on his travels away from home. If this was a criminal creature, banished or escaped from his own planet, he would be especially dangerous. And the weapon he had was able to destroy entire areas the size of Connecticut with each blast, leaving all animal life dead but mostly intact. The weapon could be fired from a distance as far as Saturn to Earth and needed incredible technology for accuracy. It was quite effective. It was mounted on a tripod or tower, and all the motion of the planet from which it was fired must be calculated in relation to the target. As you can well imagine, the process was tedious for an intelligent lizard.

The weapon had to be assembled each time the creature changed its location, and that was difficult for one person, lizard or not. The Friendlanders had calculated the time needed to assemble the weapon and had made their schedule accordingly. They had to select me from among the billions of earthlings to accomplish their mission, train me, and then allow time for travel. The complex mathematical equation, or algorithm, they used for this schedule also took into account the possibility of my lack of cooperation, if I had been so inclined, and even the selection of a replacement if I did not work out as intended. Friendland was the name of Mr. Temm's planet translated into English. This was the planet where the Adam and Eve figures remained obedient and thereby strengthened their own relationship with God rather than finding themselves cursed and thrown out like our own Adam and Eve. Mr. Temm is actually one of many grandsons of the original father, whose name was Man.

I felt like I knew everything I had ever seen or heard and then some, and it was all right there at my fingertips. I had learned much that did not seem necessary, just as Mr. Temm had said I would, such as the history of Friendland and even some personal information, like the pregnancy of Ravsen. My brain now had a large memory, and the Friendlanders had given me a ton of new technical data specifically for this mission.

I was feeling good as I flew through space. In fact, it seemed like feeling good was something I was going to have to get used to. The car ran great. They had not changed its outer appearance at all, if you just looked at it. But now it had controls where there were none before. I could give you a ride in my car and you would think it was just another car, but it was actually a space vehicle and quite loaded with extras. I figured I was going to need most of them, especially if there were to be any unexpected details on this mission. That was not likely.

The problem with space travel is not, as it turns out, the speed or even the power, but the structural stress on the vehicle. In order to accelerate to anything even close to the speed of light, the forces would smash the vehicle to bits. And, of course, because it is acceleration or deceleration that puts all the force and stress on the structure and the crew, the vehicle has to be built to withstand the forces you plan to put on it. The Camry now had its very molecular structure changed to be hard and strong enough to withstand forces, but that was only part of the solution. It also had the GAC, which stands for Gravitonic Acceleration Compensator. This amazing device uses a gravitonic field to counteract the acceleration forces as they are applied to the structure, exactly countering the effects and compensating for them. It was our own Albert Einstein that showed us how gravity and acceleration are indistinguishable from one another, but nothing on Earth has been discovered to harness or control gravity, or to copy it and create our own.

The spaceship doesn't have to be very strong to resist the loads if the loads themselves can be manipulated as they work, before they cause damage to the structure. The Friendlanders were able to create and control their own gravity, so it was a great tool to allow very fast travel through space. It's all cool stuff, but I don't want to bore you. And don't get me started on interplanetary travel.

My trip to Saturn was not really eventful, but I was fascinated by it. I made a few detours, which I later regretted, but oh, well, life is full of things to regret, so why bother? The ship was as self-piloting as possible, but it was also mine to drive as needed. The Friendlanders didn't want to send a computerized robot ship to destroy the enemy because that would be simply launching a weapon. Remember, they were not able to pull any triggers to destroy life. But by sending a pilot who had to choose to pull the trigger - well, my vehicle and I would serve nicely. I wasn't sure if I bought this story about their inability to destroy things entirely. It didn't seem to explain everything. But at the time, I figured that was due to the foreign innocence of these aliens.

I had to have a weapon, of course. Mine was not so deadly as the one the evil reptile had. Mine was about as big as the bomb that blew up Nagasaki in World War II. But there was no concern about the radiation or the loss of innocent life because there has never been any life on Dione. There is not much of anything there but rock and soil - no plants, insects, water, or air, except some gaseous stuff that oozes off the rocks and soil. The only life ever to exist on Dione would have been only the life that was capable of traveling there from other places, like this reptilian beast.

As I approached the planet Saturn, it became more and more beautiful and awesome to me. I could get used to this space-travel thing. The planet has enough color without the rings around it, but those rings have to be the most amazing thing to see in this system. And there are somewhere between eighteen and eighty satellites, depending on how you define the word "satellite." If you've seen the pictures from the exploring vessels we've sent to the planets, you can get an idea, but you should see it in 3-D and with all the motion. You would be amazed. Sorry, I digress. But the scene is amazing to behold.

I had an idea that the evil creature might have some monitors and alarms set in case anyone like me was to approach. But there were some things we knew to get around this problem. First of all, the car I was flying was very small. The alien lizard's ship was almost half as big as the Friendlander ship on the moon, but that still put it in a much larger class than my Camry. Ships that have the ability to travel to other stars need an interstellar gap-jumping apparatus, and that meant it needed more space than the Camry. We knew the configurations of his sensors, and they weren't set to see such a small craft as mine until it was right on top of him. He was only interested in ships that could distort the space continuum between stars. That's because this bad creature on Dione had no idea that any threat could come from anywhere around these parts. He must have found out as soon as he arrived on Saturn that his victims on Earth did not have the capability of coming out to chase him. The chances of a ship appearing, even like the one the Friendlanders had on the moon, was so unlikely that he probably would not consider it possible. So, the watcher was being watched, and his binoculars weren't as big as our telescope.

Nevertheless, he would know I was there if I got too close. We didn't really know what he would do if he did notice me, but he may have other weapons and things we didn't know about. You can never be sure your sensors have read everything, especially if the one you're watching wants to hide something. The Friendlanders did not at first know that other people might want to hide things at all, but they learned it from studying my people, and they began to take precautions. So we had a plan – I was to come close, but not too close.

It was all too easy, really. I just had to follow the directions, press a few buttons and switches to get my targeting calibrated, and then launch my missile once I was within a certain range. The alien creature, his spaceship, his weapon, tower and all, and all the rock and soil for many square miles around the area would all be obliterated. End of mission - go home. I could stick around to see the results of my explosion. I could even go have a look at the destruction and take a drive around the satellite, but I didn't need to. I could confirm the destruction of the life-form, and the destruction of the weapon as well, from the air-conditioned comfort of my ship.

However, one of those unexpected things happened. I did not know how important this one little glitch was going to be, and it took me by surprise. It was not in the plan, not in the schedule, and not necessarily even important. It was simply that the alien lizard's weapon discharged a sudden blast of purple energy straight in the direction of Earth. I couldn't actually see it with my eyes, but my ship's sensors were giving me information from all around. My ship's computer was programmed to alert me when something like this occurred.

It was only one blast, but it was not supposed to have happened. I determined to recheck all my monitors, the schedule, and the records before I would panic. The ghastly weapon was supposed to still be under construction. It was theoretically impossible for that weapon to discharge a blast before a certain time, but there it was. My sensors had measured the size and type of blast, and it had indeed been from the weapon on Dione.

Perhaps it was a test firing. I had to assume, to hope, that it didn't actually hit the Earth at all. What were the chances? How much damage would be done if it did? Whatever it was, I was determined to destroy this thing and accomplish this mission as soon as I could. I was not due to be in range for another twenty minutes. But that was what the preprogrammed schedule said. All I had to do was adjust my speed to get me there faster. This would compromise my secrecy a bit and make me a tiny bit more visible to the alien, if he was watching. But I decided to risk it; I had to get there sooner and launch my weapon.

I was regretting my sight-seeing detour again because I could have been to Dione hours earlier if I hadn't gone to look at Mars. But I shouldn't be so hard on myself. There was no way to predict this blast. It wasn't my fault.

I started up my targeting calibrations long before I was supposed to, according to the schedule. But I had now unofficially changed the schedule. I had to act fast. The targeting could be done while I was speeding along; it didn't matter, so I would be ready to launch at the earliest possible moment. I calculated that I could cut my time from twenty minutes to about five if I accelerated, so I began the process. The targeting was almost ready, but the computer now had to recalculate my acceleration. There. With no more course changes, the targeting would be ready when I was in range.

So, as soon as I passed the most extreme range for my missile to fly with its ultimate accuracy, I launched it. It was going to be moving a little faster than we originally planned because of my acceleration, but that was only an added bonus. I watched as the monitors showed the missile's progress, praying that there wouldn't be another blast from that evil weapon before my weapon did its work.

And then it all ended. The monster was destroyed. The evil weapon was destroyed. There had been no more blasts of energy from the alien's weapon. I breathed a great sigh of relief and was so glad this had gone well after all. I sat back and breathed deeply as I altered my course to swing around Dione. It didn't take long to get to a point where I could see the blast I had made. It was a small dot on the satellite's surface on my monitor, and it only represented the location of a great conflagration of energy, but it was gathered by sensors that told me a lot of information as I sped by on my way back around to Earth. I made sure there were no signs of life in the area or anywhere on the surface of the moon. The readings were measured as they were scheduled to be, and life had been removed from Dione. There were also readings telling me that the weapon's Elixir power source was no longer there, having been consumed in the blast. There was no spaceship, nothing except rock and soil, on Dione. I was sure of it.

I think back on that time now and I regret I didn't look closer at Dione. It has some mountains and other interesting terrain and lots of craters, of course, but that isn't too exciting. The system data Mr. Temm had given me showed Dione to have a bit of a troubling contrast with hot, volcanic violence erupting into a cold, frozen fume of poison. Yes, I should have taken a closer look at Dione, but I was distracted by my own version of volcanic activity quickly cooling in the void of my own small soul.

Mission accomplished. But I did not feel like celebrating. I felt sick.

Chapter 8 - The Fall

As I headed back to the Friendland ship on Earth's moon, I recomposed myself and thought through the whole affair. It was now late into Sunday, and I was wondering if I was going to miss my Black Belt test. Surely I could be home before next Saturday. I assumed everyone thought I was either dead or kidnapped. My picture was probably on the news as a mystery to everyone. Actually, who was I kidding? I could be just taking a rest over a long weekend. No one would even notice I was gone, except I hadn't shown up for work on Friday.

That wasn't bothering me very much right then. If anyone, either at my job or at church or in Taekwon-Do class were to ask where I'd been, what was I going to tell them? Surely no one would believe the truth. But I had not forgotten Mr. Temm's promise to reward me for the great action I had performed on behalf of his people. I was going to make sure I received enough payment to cover any inconveniences that were probably in store for me. As I flew back, it seemed very likely that I was going to be in some very inconvenient trouble when I got home.

Maybe I could just go back home with the aliens to their planet. The Earth could do without me. Maybe I would be famous on Friendland. But that was no consolation to me. I didn't even want to visit that planet, where there was fruit to eat all year around and water to drink around every corner. No, they probably didn't even have corners on the whole planet. Anyway, it would be impossible for me to be gone from my wife and kids. I was missing them more and more, and I had been trying not to think about them too much. Thinking of them just reminded me that I missed them and needed them. I hoped they weren't having too much fun without me.

But surely Mr. Temm would listen if I asked for his help. He could straighten out any mess with my life back home, couldn't he? Hadn't he said he would give me whatever I wanted? He can cover for me somehow so I won't have to lie my way through the rest of my life. I was so eager to see my new greenish blue friends again so we could celebrate, and they could send me home. So what if I miss the test, and maybe I won't. I'm just happy to be alive!

I should be more concerned about missing my wife at the airport on Wednesday. She would call from the airport, wondering where I was, and eventually would have to hire a taxi to get home. And what am I going to say? That I was busy doing a favor for some new friends who had stopped by the moon on their vacation? And by the way, I would've picked you up at the airport, but I had to run an errand on Saturn? I think she would see to it that I got some good psychological counseling after she divorced me.

These were the things running through my head as I traveled back to Mr. Temm's ship. Then, after some stewing on these unhappy possibilities, I tried to be hopeful. I tried to think realistically. My wife will be glad to see me. It worked out well that she and the kids were gone out of town when this all happened to me. What a coincidence. That should make it easier for me to cover any questions. I began the deceleration for my arrival to the moon.

But when I got closer to the moon, I began getting readings that were not what I expected. There was something going on. The ship was not on the moon anymore. Oh, it was there, but it was now floating in orbit instead of on the surface, where the schedule said it should be. It looked like they were leaving. What was the hurry? Friendlanders never hurry.

I drifted into the docking bay and went looking for Mr. Temm. The power fields were in working order, keeping the interior of the ship protected from the vacuum of space, but everything was wrong. There were no people around. There should have been someone here to greet me. They all knew what I had done, where I was. They should have known. I figured I would start in the main part of the ship where so much of the usual activities of life were usually spent during waking hours. I knew all about the ship, as it had been part of my training. That was some of that extra data I might need but was not necessarily part of the planned mission, so I was able to go straight there.

I burst into the large room, and there was Mr. Temm, alone, as if he was driving the huge ship like a captain. He was not driving the ship, of course, but he had his sight off into the distance of starry space. He spoke without turning. "Hello, Demetrius. I saw that you returned. I have waited for you."

"What's going on? What has happened?" He was slow to respond.

"We do not know exactly what the particular action was. Maybe it was a single thought or a single moment of weakness. Perhaps it was not just one of us, but many of us. Or all of us."

He wasn't making sense, but he was calm. He seemed more lonely than I had ever seen him. He looked different. "What has happened to your clothes, your hair?" He was disheveled, as if he had been in a fight. I had never seen him in anything but his clean, immaculate clothes and neatly cut hair, but now it was all messy, and he was grimy with soil and sweat. I could smell it. I knew the smell of sweat. "Tell me. What do you need? What has happened?"

He turned to face me. He looked ashamed. He must have been crying. That seemed impossible because these people never cried. "Our Lord God has departed from us. One of us...some of us...all of us...have sinned."

I was not shocked. I was trying to think on my feet and think fast, because the ship didn't seem right. I thought we were going to crash. "Listen to me! I can help you. You must not lose hope." This crazy swirling would probably have been impossible for me to handle, but I had Mr. Temm's gift in my brain and body, and I was able to think fast and calculate the implications of what was happening. "You must not lose hope! God has not abandoned you. He did not abandon us, and he will not abandon you! You must listen!"

I felt a great lurch as the ship started to go off where it didn't belong. As I caught my balance, I saw that Mr. Temm had simply sat down in his big chair when the jolt hit. He didn't look like he was going anywhere. I would have to deal with him later. I had to get this ship back in order. Someone had abandoned his post.

I had only been trained to fly the one small ship, but the knowledge was good for understanding other ships too. I would not be able to pilot this huge vessel, but I knew something about what kept it flying right. So, I went to the control room. The people who should have been operating things were nowhere to be seen. Surely there were going to be consequences and repercussions for abandoning their posts, but maybe not. This was not a human group. I went to the controls and did what I could. I had to go by feel and sound, as there were no specific markings or writings to guide me. And I couldn't have read them if they existed. I got things to stabilize fairly easily. It was not so difficult a task. This was the simple stuff that had to be done every day while the ship was in flight. The simple fact that no one was doing anything at all to maintain the status was what concerned me most. Anyone on the ship could have most likely done the job.

I did have to do the jobs of about four or five people, but the area was not too difficult to negotiate, and the timing was no special thing once you put your mind to it. I wondered where everybody was. Mr. Temm had said that someone, or maybe more than one of them, sinned. Why would that happen so suddenly? I wondered.

And he said God had departed from them. Get used to it. I had never seen God in my life. That didn't mean he wasn't there.

As I went back to speak to Mr. Temm, I felt that sick feeling I had noticed when the mission had been accomplished. I had never actually killed anyone before. I never was in the military, and I never got into any accidents or fights where anyone actually died. But that creature was an evil lizard, wasn't he? He was cruelly and viciously murdering populations just because he could. Well, it was none of my business. The Friendlanders needed this creature gone, and the people on Earth had been saved. There was no way I could have stopped that creature without killing him, killing it.

I found Mr. Temm where I had left him. Now I had to get through to him. "Look, you may be guilty of sin, but it doesn't mean God left you. He doesn't do that. Surely you have studied the Earth people, my people, long enough to see that there is still much hope. You have seen how many of us find God again after we get tired of living without him." I had started off quietly and calmly, but I felt myself get emotional as I continued, perhaps even angry.

But I didn't seem to be having any effect on Mr. Temm. We both remained silent while I tried to think of what to say next.

"Mr. Temm, these people are all going to die if you don't take charge and help them. You have a responsibility. You are their leader."

He looked at me. After a while he said, "On your planet everyone knows they are going to die, so why do they fight it so hard? It seems easy now for me to just get it over with. Why should I fight? It just doesn't matter."

"Yes, it does matter! Can you be so sure that all forty-seven of your friends are ready to die? Do they know that God is able to forgive them or that there is still hope for them? They need to know that they can meet together with all the ones who have died when the end of the age comes. Do *you* know it? You must stay alive long enough to make sure every one of them finds God again, now that they've lost him. You know God is still there – you must tell them. They will believe you. Don't let them die if there is another chance."

"You tell them, Mr. Adrien."

"No! You are their leader, they need you! How many of them are your children, your grandchildren? They will listen to you. I am not their savior; you are. It's why we're all here, so you can see how we've dealt with it on my planet. We still have hope, and so can you."

"Why did God go away?"

"Listen to me! God had to go away because he must be invisible. Otherwise, faith has no value. If God is visible, then there is no need to believe in him. But if God stays hidden, then your free will is indeed free to believe or to not believe. It will be your choice, and therefore, it will be valuable. There is no such thing as love unless you have the ability to choose not to love. He loves you."

I knew that logic was not going to win any arguments to get someone to believe in God, so I began to quiet myself down. I needed to let Mr. Temm think, and I needed to pray for him. I said one more thing, "God sent his own son to our planet to be tortured and killed so that we would not have to be. He was innocent and did not deserve to die. But God knew that only such a devastating thing could redeem all of us. His own son had to die for us. So we can be forgiven if we just ask.

"I think that same Jesus you read about in our Bible has also died for you, Mr. Temm." And I stopped talking and prayed. That was good for me also.

He seemed to hear all that I said, but I wasn't sure if he cared. But eventually he did a good thing. He turned and noticed the state of the ship. He realized that the engines weren't operating. He ran and started banging on doors. He started acting like a heroic earthling, like a sinner from Earth who understands that he has some form of responsibility. When the other green people were shocked out of their stupor, he spoke to them in their own language. I was still unable to understand it. He had not given me the ability to speak their own language during my training. While we were going through the ship, I counted the people we encountered. Eventually we got to number forty-seven, and I felt great relief as that last one woke up and ran off to his ordered duty.

So, Mr. Temm *had* heard my voice, and he now knew why I was here - not to destroy an alien with a weapon, not to give him and his forty-seven friends a new hope, but to teach him what to do when he fell, to teach him how to get up and go find God when God has moved away a bit because he can't stand to be around you right then. I was there to make his fall easier than mine had been, and he knew it. Somehow, he knew it. He became restored to God's side like I had, long after I was born into a cruel world. It would never be like it was before, but it could be good again.

Mr. Temm got his ship stabilized and back on course. What I had done may have helped, but the ship needed more, that's for sure. He got his companions to get up and work, and he got his dignity back, or maybe he found dignity for the first time. It took some hours, but the confusion finally ended. There were tears, there was anger, and there was laughter, all in a place where they had never been before. These people had watched planet Earth so long that they knew more about sin than we earthlings did. Once they committed their own sin, God was there to forgive them, and they all knew it, once Mr. Temm had reminded them.

I never knew exactly what sin they committed nor who committed it. It's none of my business.

Mr. Temm seemed to think I needed to leave soon, and that my job was done. I wasn't sure if I had done anything really but survive through another weekend saving one planet while ruining another. The truth is, I was afraid to think about what I might discover if I sat down to consider all that had just happened.

I had seen the fall of Adam and Eve, but it was forty-eight people in a spaceship. They happened to stumble upon a planet in their innocent travels, and that planet had taught them what they would have been better off without learning about humans. I kept telling myself it wasn't my fault. But I couldn't separate myself from the events that had happened. And I kept telling myself it wasn't an entire population, but only these forty-eight wandering souls. And I kept telling myself they weren't condemned to Hell. God could forgive them just as he forgave us - forgave me, a long time ago.

Mr. Temm and his baby were going to have a hard road to travel now. But they had all of human history and resources to learn from. Maybe they would be all right. I wanted so badly to go home. But I also wanted to stay with my green-skinned friends. They needed me. No. They have Mr. Temm. He's a good man. They don't need me.

"Are you going to try to go back to Friendland?"

"No. I think you know we cannot go there, Demetrius. They who live there can do without us."

"It is ironic, isn't it? You have learned so much."

"But look at the price. We cannot say that a world where God must remain invisible to the people is better than a world where sin has never set foot. Faith in an invisible God is good only because there is no other choice. He cannot show himself to those he hopes to save. Their faith must be of their own free will, and he must be invisible for faith and love to have meaning." These words were all his own now. I wondered if he remembered where he had learned them. But he continued.

"We cannot risk the consequences of our sin entering into our entire world's population. We will find a home elsewhere. We already have seen some planets that might do nicely where we could not harm anyone.

"Come, I must send you back where you came from."

My car was back in the living room where I had first entered this whole thing. That room was in fact a room for transporting materials to and from other locations, like the surfaces of planets. All I had to do was get back in my car, and Mr. Temm would send me back to Earth. But there were a couple more things to do before I left.

"Mr. Adrien, you were wrong about one thing." His voice was more human now. He had some emotion that was causing him to stay quieter than he needed to be. I think he was embarrassed.

"No way. What was I wrong about?"

"Earlier you spoke as if I had forty-seven friends on this ship. But I have forty-eight."

I felt the compliment. I knew he wasn't talking about his wife's unborn baby. I decided not to respond, but maybe I couldn't have anyway if I had tried.

"My friend, I have given you a gift, or actually gifts, which I hope you will be pleased by. I believe it is a good thing for me not to explain them to you, but let you be surprised when you find them instead. I hope you will consider my personal thanks to have value also.

"We should not meet again, Mr. Adrien. The technology we possess is something we will have to learn to control, and your people are not ready for our science. I hope you understand that." It was at this time that Ravsen entered. She looked somewhat different, but I wasn't sure why. I supposed it may have been the sin.

"I have come to say good-bye, Mr. Adrien, and I also wish to thank you. It is difficult to know how to do so because what you have done is new to me. So much is new to me. I do not like much of it, but there is still hope. Our new son may one day perhaps accomplish something." She turned and left, and I realized, suddenly, that she was talking about dying. These people were all going to die now, each in his own day, and they knew it. It was something new.

Now it was my turn to weep.

Chapter 9 - Home When?

When Mr. Temm saw the tears in my eyes, he looked at me more deeply than he ever had before. There was an understanding, a sad kinship, between us now. We understood each other more than we had wanted. We shared our disgust with our own races of people, which made us equal now.

We also knew about value. Mr. Temm indicated that he wanted me to get into the car, and he walked away. But I knew he was coming back. When he did, he looked like a man with a secret. He came to the car and shook my hand before I got into it. There was no need for more words. He knew we understood each other too well. *Let's get this over with*, we were both thinking. So, I sat in my car. I didn't start the ignition. I knew better. I knew how to operate this vehicle with my brain full of new data making me a different man than the one who had come here a few days ago. My heart was full of some new things as well.

I sat back and waited. There was nothing else left. Now I had to get ready to face the music at the other end of this final trip. Was I going back to that parking garage? I guess Mr. Temm could place me and my car anywhere he wanted.

I felt nothing as the walls disappeared, and the parking garage came into focus around me. It was just as dark and quiet as I remembered it. I was sitting still, not moving. The engine was not running. I just sat there and looked around to verify that I was really back.

Someone honked a horn. I jumped and realized that I was blocking traffic. So I started up the engine and moved out of the way. I continued driving and exited the parking garage, thinking it didn't really matter where I went or how much time I wasted trying to decide what to do next. If I had been gone three or four days, what difference would it make if I waited another hour? So, I began driving toward home.

I made my way through parking lots back out to the highway frontage road. There seemed to be some sort of holdup in traffic. Oh, there, it was a semi-trailer truck that had stopped. I sat back and remembered I was in no hurry. I was in a parking lot anyway, so I just made sure I wasn't blocking traffic this time, and I sat back to rest and rolled down the window.

I was struck immediately with the smell of that semi-trailer truck's brakes. I had seen this same truck when it skidded almost off the road last Thursday! Could this be Thursday still, or again, or what?

I immediately moved to find a back way out of this parking lot and made my way down a couple of back roads. I knew that I could get on my cross street without having to get in the highway traffic, and I was on my way. My watch was still reading the time as if it was four days after Thursday, but my hopes were that Mr. Temm had taken me not just back to Earth, not just back to where I came from, but also back to *when* I came from. Could it be? I drove a little bit faster than usual while watching for police cars. I seemed to be more aware than when I had been here last. My senses were reeling as I realized everything was back to normal again, but I had been to Saturn and the moon. I wouldn't have to explain anything to anyone if it were still Thursday. Thank you, Mr. Temm!

I arrived at Taekwon-Do class, and there were cars there as usual. Everything was looking normal. If this was Sunday, there would be no cars here. Or was it Monday already? I was not sure what day it was because I didn't care what day it was. I wanted it to be Thursday again. I was getting more excited than ever as I entered the training center. Mr. Halyard was teaching the first class, so I went into the restroom to change into my uniform. Everything was going so well that I stopped to thank God. The biggest problem I thought I was going to have was explaining where I had been for three days, and now I didn't have to do that. This must be Thursday. Was it possible that this was Monday? I had to find out. I changed into my *do bok* and walked out to join the class as usual. If I had been gone for three or four days, surely someone would say something.

There were parents and little kids around as usual while their sons and daughters and brothers and sisters practiced their *sa-bhang* drills with one of the young Black Belts. Mr. Halyard had four First Degree Black Belts who acted as assistant instructors. They were learning how to teach now that they were no longer just students. I bowed and said, "Tae Kwon," before stepping out on the padded floor. If anyone had been surprised to see me, there was no comment and no staring. Just the same looks I might have normally received. Mr. Halyard smiled at me and gave a slight bow of acknowledgement. Normally, those of us who wore red belts would not be allowed to enter in until it was time for our class, but he had been letting me help teach some classes along with the Black Belts. I assumed that was because I was in my thirties already and the Black Belts were all teenagers or college students.

Mr. Halyard came over and shook my hand when he got a free moment. "Good to see you, Mr. Adrien."

"Thank you, sir. It's good to be here."

"I'm going to need your help as much as possible all next week to prepare people for testing. Can you be here this Saturday?"

So, it was definitely still Thursday. He was asking me to come in to help on the Saturday before testing. I was ecstatic. "Yes, sir. That should be no problem. My wife and the kids aren't expected back from Seattle until Wednesday, so my time is a bit more free."

"Good. I may not be able to rely on the First Degrees because of their school schedules this week, so your help will be very welcome."

The first two classes were for the lower ranks. First was the class for the White Belts, or Tenth Gup students, up through the rank of Seventh Gup, and then was the class for the Sixth Gup Green Belts up to the rank of Third Gup. I helped out by taking whichever group Mr. Halyard gave me and working with them on their material. They would not be testing for a few more weeks because the Black Belt tests were always done separately from the Gup tests. The event when Black Tab Red Belts were tested for promotion to Black Belt only happened twice a year. The colored belt grades had a test every month, but they weren't due for a few weeks.

The third class of the evening was for Red Belts and Black Belts only. I was interested to see how my body would perform with all of the repair work Mr. Temm had done in my training. I felt good, and I wouldn't have any trouble remembering the movements of the patterns and drills down to the smallest detail. But I wanted to feel it, and I was eager to begin class.

And I was not disappointed. It felt good to do patterns. In order to become a Black Belt, one had to perform all the patterns for all the Gup ranks up to my level, Red Belt with Black Tab, or First Gup. Some students pay more attention to their newest pattern and neglect the old ones when they learn their new one, but I had always tried to practice the old ones as well. But now, as I went through the patterns with the rest of the group, I felt like I might not need to practice anymore. I felt like I could teach myself now. I thought that Taekwon-Do was going to be easier than I had ever thought possible.

The beginning of class was always spent getting the students warmed up with stretching exercises, and even then I felt more flexible than ever, thanks to Mr. Temm. I had never been able to do the full splits with both legs spread wide all the way down to the floor. But that Thursday evening, when I realized I was going to be able to do the splits, I began a trend that I later regretted. I held back and pretended that I was still the same old Demetrius. I began to deceive everyone, or so I thought, as if I were afraid they would notice I had changed and I would have to explain myself.

I assumed that my new abilities to stretch farther, to jump higher, and to perform better would all need to appear to be slow changes to not make anyone suspicious about why I was suddenly so much better. Little did I know that I would have been better off just doing my best. At the time, I thought maybe I was going to be so good at Taekwon-Do that I may not need an instructor, or maybe I could teach Mr. Halyard a few things, if he would listen.

I knew I was going to have to figure some things out. I believed that God had answered the prayer I had prayed on my way home from work for so many weeks, but I still didn't know exactly what to do with myself. How was I supposed to take these new qualities of mine and use them for the right purpose? I had some thinking and sorting out to do. Maybe this whole thing wasn't over yet.

Chapter 10 - Mr. Temm's Gifts

On the way home, I stopped by the bank. I needed some cash, which was a bit unusual, but because my wife was away for a few more days I would continue living like a bachelor and would need to take care of myself. I got the usual $40 out of the ATM, and I started to pocket the receipt so we would have a record of the withdrawal. But as I glanced at it, I saw too many digits.

There was no one around because it was after 10:00 P.M. The only noise was from the cars on the roadway. As I looked at that bank statement, I was utterly amazed. The slip of paper always included the available balance in the account, and so it did this time. But this bank account now had enough money in it for me to stop working for about three years! That was impossible.

I knew – hoped – that Mr. Temm had somehow made this happen and that it was not a bank error. But wait, this was still Thursday. Mr. Temm had not yet made me the promise to give me a reward. When I returned to Earth, I had traveled back in time to the moment before all that crazy space travel had happened. But, wait. What was going on up there on the moon right now? If I calculated correctly, I was there on the moon discussing things with Mr. Temm and Ravsen, right now on Thursday evening. I must be in two places at one time, here and on the moon.

Well, because Mr. Temm and his people knew how to time travel, then I supposed he knew how to put something in my bank account in the past. This was zany, and my head was starting to hurt thinking about it. I still had the car that could travel to Saturn. I still had the super-sensitive eyes, ears, nose, and skin. I was able to recall the weights and distances of all the planets with extreme accuracy. The memories of all that had happened were very real, and I was still maintaining all the training and repair work I had gone through. I was going to have to check with the bank tomorrow and check the true balance of my bank account. That gave me an excuse to stay home from work, anyway. I hadn't used any of my paid sick time yet this year.

I drove home and put the car in the garage, as usual. It struck me as funny that the remote control for the garage door had been in the car the whole time I was away on the moons and planets and that it still worked to open the garage door as it had always done. I wasn't looking for there to be any surprises when I got home, and indeed everything looked normal enough.

I got out of the car, went to the door, and never thought to look around the garage. If I had, I would have seen that some improvements had been made. I stepped through and turned to lock the garage before stepping up to the front door of the house. I noticed my front door was different.

There were a number of differences about the house, actually. I found them all eventually, but I saw the front door first. There was the same porch with the light on, the same bench, and the same potted plants decorating the area. But now the door was freshly painted. I noticed this because it had needed painting for some time now.

And there was a sort of key pad there where there had never been one before. It was not a key pad, because there were no buttons on it, just a sort of panel above the normal keyhole. I reached for the door handle, and the latch was unlocked. I seemed to have been trained to understand how this door worked. The door had a sensor that recognized it was me. I also knew that my wife could still use her key to unlock the door as she always did.

This was a weird detail because I was going to have some secrets from my wife, whether I liked it or not. Maybe someday I could tell her the story, but I couldn't imagine how that would ever happen. Maybe I could take her to visit Mr. Temm someday.

Needless to say, I was now interested to find out what else was different around here, and I was not disappointed. The whole house was remodeled and beautiful. There was white marble on the family room floor and new wood baseboards and banisters leading up the stairway, creating a wonderful contrast. All the old carpet was gone and replaced by wood flooring in some places and various types of tiles in others. The furniture was relocated, repaired, and cleaned up, with some new pieces added here and there.

There were computer upgrades at all four of our desks, a new television - new everything. The kitchen was redone even better than my wife and I had ever discussed and dreamed. There was still food in the new refrigerator, and much of it was new.

I explored my own house in wonder and then decided that Mr. Temm was getting good at his newly learned gift-giving. Everything upstairs and down was wonderful. My wife was going to love this. I was sure she would love this, wasn't I?

I panicked for a moment as I thought of her again. She would need to know how all this came about and where I got the money for everything. I was going to be in deep trouble. No, she would love it. I was suddenly tired of panic, tired of being scared about what others might think, even my wife. She was just going to love this. That's all there was to it.

I slept well that night, and I didn't set the alarm.

But I did wake early enough to call in to work. I had an important errand to run at the bank. I found out that one account from which I had withdrawn $40 was only one of seven accounts we had at this bank. The total amount of money we had was more than I had ever thought Mr. Temm was going to give me. I thought the lady I spoke with at the bank seemed a bit stuffy for a Friday, but when I started to laugh out of happiness and joy, she seemed to gain something from it. Her own laughter may have been directly at me, but I didn't care.

That afternoon I went through the house in more detail and tried to find everything new. At some point in the middle of the day I called my wife because I remembered she was scheduled to have a short day on Friday and she would be back at her mom's house early. I tried to sound cheerful and hinted that I had a surprise for her when she got home. I actually had no idea what I was going to tell her about the money, but I had stopped worrying about it. I was ready to just take whatever consequences came, no matter what. The burden of worry was gone from my shoulders. It was definitely gone. Somehow everything would all work out.

After I spent the day looking through the house and becoming familiar with the new things, I sat on the back porch as the sun set and prayed my heart to God, thankful that I was alive and things had worked out like they had. I remembered the vague prayer I had prayed in my car and that he had answered so completely and amazingly. I still wondered why it was *me* that had been chosen for this crazy turn of events. Surely I wasn't the best suited for heroism among all the billions of people on Earth. Oh, well, the mysteries of the universe were not mine to understand.

After I finished my prayer, I looked up at the stars, and there was the moon. I was there right now also. No, I was on my way to Saturn right now in my souped-up Toyota. If my calculations were correct, I was just now having a good look at Deimos as it swung past the near surface of Mars. Perhaps I shouldn't have made that detour, but it was certainly fascinating.

I still had a question, but asking it didn't seem to matter. My prayer for the evening had finished, and only God could answer this one. He had answered the prayer I had prayed repeatedly for almost six weeks, and it was all over now, or was it? I was content this evening.

I smiled as I spoke aloud to the moon, "What am I going to do now?"

Part 2 – My Own Mission

Chapter 11 - Got Purpose?

On Saturday I was back at Taekwon-Do class. We always had the best class on Saturday. It was for Red and Black Belts only, and it lasted two hours. After the opening warm-ups and stretches, we were going to do all our patterns, and then we would do whatever drills and training Mr. Halyard had in store for us. One good thing about this school was that there was never a dull moment. Even the kids didn't get bored because every class was different, and there was always something new coming up.

I was going to test for Black Belt in one week. I never felt better as I performed that day, doing every movement as if I was incapable of making a mistake. Some of the techniques I had found difficult before were no longer a problem. Even the timing of the scooping blocks in *Toi-gae* pattern had improved. And I seemed to never tire of the bag work. It seemed like I could kick and punch all day. After the two-hour class, I was ready for more, and I kept my promise to help teach the next two classes. Just as Mr. Halyard had predicted, the Black Belts were not reliable today as assistants. Only one was able to stay to help teach after the first class. The others had things to do, and I thought they looked too tired after their workout anyway.

But during class I had watched the Black Belts do their patterns when the rest of us had been dismissed to practice on our own. As I was getting a drink from my water bottle, I wondered if I could learn a pattern just by watching it. I knew we weren't supposed to learn patterns from the ranks higher than our own, but it couldn't hurt to just watch, could it? That one they were doing called *Po-eun* seemed rather easy to learn actually. I think they did eighteen movements to the right side and then repeated the same eighteen movements to the left side with the opposite hand and foot. I thought I wouldn't have any trouble learning that when the time came.

When I went home to my new place – well, it felt new now even though I had lived there for eight years – the sky was cloudy and there was a smell of rain in the air. It looked like everything was normal, even the weather. As it started to rain, I was tinkering with the computer Mr. Temm had given me. It looked like there were some new and seriously high-tech programs on this machine. When I checked the other computers, which belonged to my family members, it seemed that theirs were more normal than mine. They had the latest and greatest software and hardware, but they lacked some of the extra stuff mine had. It was going to take some time to get the full picture about this computer. I assumed a lot of the necessary instruction was in my head as part of my training. Good, I wouldn't have to read the manual.

On Sunday after church I had lunch with some friends from Bible class. After that, I sat down to turn on the TV when I got home, and I rubbed my hands. They were still sore from punching on the heavy bag, which I had done the day before in Taekwon-Do class. That was okay, I just needed to take it easy next time. I had already noticed my feet had some redness on the top where I had done a lot of hard turning kicks to the kicking bag. So, as invulnerable as I felt with my new, repaired body, I was still human, and I needed to take some care to not overdo it in the physical training.

There was nothing much to watch as I flipped through the TV channels. Oh, there were lots of shows and lots of interesting things to see and hear, but I had not been in the habit of watching television since I got out of college. I had always had things to do to keep me busy, like Taekwon-Do, reading both fiction and non-fiction, studying chess, and other things, so I seldom sat down and got to know the characters on the tube.

Even though I now had hundreds of channels to choose from, I stopped flipping the remote on the afternoon news program of a local station. As the news went on much like it does every day, I almost fell asleep on the nice, new couch. It seemed like a good idea to just let myself doze off. But eventually I heard something that had me up and awake as fast as ever.

"There were nineteen people killed today in Seattle, Washington, from what the police are calling a meteorite fallen from space. We'll tell you the details after these commercial messages." When I heard "Seattle," I sat up straight. I couldn't believe there could be something falling from space to Seattle of all places, right where my wife and kids were visiting relatives. And wouldn't you know it, but the news commentator actually went to a different story before telling more details about the Seattle meteorite. But finally, I turned up the volume as they told of the tragic deaths of nineteen people.

"It was uncertain why the meteorite left no remnants and why there were no damaged buildings or automobiles. And strangely enough, there were no other injuries reported aside from the nineteen who were found dead at the scene of a shopping mall parking lot in Seattle. There were a number of calls to the 911 emergency lines reporting a variety of things. One caller thought it was an explosion and feared that terrorists had struck the shopping mall. Other callers reported fire, lightning, and even an earthquake. No one seemed to agree what caused the huge cloud of smoky dust until scientists suggested that a meteorite might have burned its way through the Earth's atmosphere, only to leave fire, dust, and smoke to come crashing into the parking lot as it expended its final energy. This would possibly explain why the victims were not noticeably burned or otherwise outwardly injured, as the thick dust could have actually suffocated the victims, knocking the wind out of them and leaving no air to breathe, rather than physically destroying their bodies. The snow piled around the area showed no signs of melting, however, as the winter temperatures remain near freezing.

"The authorities are asking anyone who may have filmed the phenomenon with a home video camera to please call in so their footage can aid the investigation of this unusual occurrence.

"The nineteen victims have not been identified, but we will keep you informed of further developments as the investigation continues. We will have an update in our evening news report tonight at 10:00 P.M."

My jaw dropped, and my mouth hung open as my eyes glazed over. I somehow knew that my wife and two children were part of that nineteen. Why? No, it couldn't be. I couldn't know something like that. There must be thousands of people in Seattle or millions. Not *my* family. No, it couldn't be. I would stay calm, have some dinner, and wait patiently for the ten o'clock news. Surely I was mistaken. It had to be a coincidence.

Lightning? Meteorite? No injured people in the area, only dead ones? From space? When?

What was going on right now on the satellites of Saturn? There was a lizard-like monster with an Elixir electro-proton weapon. A Toyota Camry was flying toward it a bit too casually to put an end to the monster and his weapon. One purple burst from that gun would take over an hour to reach Earth if it traveled at the speed of light. What time had that been? Sunday at 2:45 P.M. That was only a few hours ago. If it hit around 4:00 P.M., which was only 2:00 P.M. in Seattle, they could have had it on the 5:00 P.M. news. My wife had said they were going shopping on Sunday.

I did not have to wait for the news at ten o'clock. I got a telephone call. Three of the victims of the "meteorite" had been from Texas: a woman and her son and daughter. My wife. My family. Now I knew why it had been me that Mr. Temm chose. It had been me because I was not going to be missed once my family was dead and gone. Mr. Temm knew that I had been in great danger after all, and he didn't even expect me to return from Saturn.

No.

Mr. Temm could not possibly have known that my wife and kids were going to be killed. Three days after he called me and offered me the chance to save my planet? No way! What was going on here? This is too outrageous. The odds were too great against this happening. I supposed only God could do this. Had my prayer been answered or not?

I did a lot of praying, even for me, after that. The Black Belt test was postponed until further notice. The funeral and memorial services were all taken care of expediently. It was a few days before I sat alone again. Everyone who had ever known me came to be my friend in my time of loss, and I was only alone to sleep. My dreams were stormy nightmares of space and asteroids and purple lightning and thunder, dusty thunder.

This was not fair, and it was not an answered prayer. I was mad. And God knew who I was mad at. I sat and stormed within myself, but in the direction of God, who must have been trying to play games with me. I was trying to decide whether to yell actual words or just to scream sounds of fury, but what happened was somewhat quieter.

God apologized.

That is exactly how it felt when I finally cried. It felt like God apologized for the trouble he had had to put me through. This was not his fault. He was still God, not any different than before. I was the only one playing games, childish games. The only noises were my sobbing and blubbering.

But eventually, with wet cheeks and red eyes, I smiled feebly as I realized I could do something about this. I knew how to travel back in time, and I was going to go back and destroy that lizard about thirty minutes earlier than I had the first time, before the stupid weapon fired that blast.

Chapter 12 - Monty

There was a lot to do in the next few days, or so I thought. It was already Wednesday again before I had time to relax and decide what to do. Now I needed to start going through a checklist of the things I needed to accomplish during this new mission.

I had not been to Taekwon-Do class since Saturday, but I hoped to go tomorrow. Maybe Mr. Halyard would reschedule the Black Belt test. And it would feel good to sweat again and to work out. But here it was Wednesday evening, and I was not about to go to bed early. I went to the garage.

I did not really know how to go back in time, at least not exactly. But I knew it could be done, and I had every intention of doing it again. I just had to tap all of my resources. The car had a computer in it with a lot of information, so that's where I decided to start.

The garage was nice and clean, which was a new look for this garage. We had had too much stuff stored in it, and the place didn't get swept out and made neat as often as it needed. But now the car fit well into its neat garage, and the car itself was neater than it used to be. I knew that I would never have to wash this car again because it had a special feature that polarized dust particles every so often and caused them to push away from the vehicle. I noticed that the dents and dings, which I had snickered at before, were slowly repairing themselves. The car was quite smooth now.

I would also never need to add gasoline again, as the new power source was going to last longer than my lifetime. I vaguely wondered how I was going to get the car inspected next October, which was required in the state of Texas every year. I would worry about that later. It would not surprise me if the inspection sticker updated itself with the help of Mr. Temm's magic.

I got in the car and started looking up things in the records. I wanted to get in touch with Mr. Temm first, if I could. The communications system was there to use, but I had not needed it yet. I flipped the switches to get the correct settings for his big craft and said, "Mr. Temm, do you read me?" But there was no answer. He had obviously left the moon by now and was on his way to find a new home. I switched off the communicator and said, "So long, Mr. Temm. Good luck."

I actually jumped, believe it or not, because a voice spoke. "He cannot hear you with the system turned off, and he is out of range, nevertheless." It was not Mr. Temm's voice. It was coming from the dashboard or the speakers or from all around me.

I responded, "Who are you?"

The voice said, "Ship's computer."

This was going to be convenient. Perhaps I was not going to have to read through the whole library to find what I wanted. "You can speak?"

"Yes."

The voice was not a real person's voice, of course. I knew that. But I soon found myself thinking of the computer as a person. I guess I considered the whole car to be a person, really. It was not like Mr. Temm's voice, and it was not Ravsen's voice, but perhaps it sounded a little like both of them to me.

"Computer, I have a few questions for you."

"I will answer."

"Do you remember when we returned here to Earth, how the time of day and the day itself were not what I expected?"

"Yes. I have all the information in my memory."

"Computer, do you understand that we did something that I will call time travel that I have never heard of anyone doing before? In fact, Computer, did you know that time travel is considered impossible by the people of this planet?"

"Yes. I understand. Yes. I know."

This computerized voice was going to take some getting used to. I especially needed to remember not to speak to the car if I ever had a human passenger. No, wait. It was okay for me to speak to the car, but not for the car to speak back. "Computer. I have a, um, a command for you. I want you to hide your own identity. Hide your own existence from all other people besides me. Can you do that?"

"Yes. It has already been decided that the people of your planet will not learn about me, nor will they learn about the differences of this car and others. You do not need to concern yourself with this matter, Mr. Adrien. I am programmed to never reveal myself to anyone else, even if you command me otherwise."

"Who programmed you?"

"Mr. Temm and Mr. Chamm."

I had never learned the names of any of the other forty-six members of the crew of Mr. Temm's ship. That seemed rather sad. But I supposed none of them had learned English, so it wasn't possible for me to talk with them anyway. Still, a name or two might have been nice.

"By the way, Computer, you can call me Demetrius, or simply Demetri, if you wish."

"Thank you, Demetrius. You can call me Monty."

I nearly laughed out loud. I probably should have. Was I afraid of hurting the computer's feelings? "Thanks, Monty.

"Could you instruct me how to make a time machine that will allow me to travel back in time, like we did before?"

"Yes."

Great. I breathed a sigh of relief as I got closer to my goal. I had to find a way of bringing my wife and kids back, or I would die trying. I realized, as I sat there in the car that night, that I had not had a successful mission after all. I may have saved the planet, but not completely. Nineteen people had died, and that meant I had not saved the whole planet. I wondered how I would feel if three of those nineteen had not been my own family members. I regretted to admit that I may not have noticed those nineteen if they had just been any other nineteen people. I wouldn't have been so enthusiastic if it had been a bunch of strangers. I supposed I was typical in that way.

Well, I was glad that those other sixteen were going to benefit as well along with their friends and loved ones. Maybe fifty or more people would actually be affected. I needed to accomplish this. And it was possible.

"How long will it take to build this time machine, Monty?"

"Approximately fourteen weeks, Demetrius."

What? That was three and a half months. Could I wait that long? This was not good news. "Will I be able to use this time machine to travel back to the time, say, two days before the alien creature was destroyed on Dione?" I assumed the time machine could be set to go anywhere, anytime, that I wanted to travel.

But Monty said, "No."

I wasn't sure I believed this talking computer. What was the problem now? "Why not?"

"One cannot travel to a time before the time distortion device existed."

"So, if the time machine was built and started up on May 26th, then I could not travel to a time before May 26th?" I thought this was crazy and not fair. But it made sense.

"That is correct, Demetrius."

I was starting to lose hope, and it was still only Wednesday. "Monty, is there any way I can travel back to that time when the alien was destroyed on Dione?"

"Yes."

My hope was jump-started. "How?"

"Mr. Chamm has equipped this vehicle with a time displacement system. We can go back to the 16th of February whenever you wish, Demetrius."

I was ecstatic. I didn't need to build a new time machine. This computer probably knew everything I needed to know, but I just wasn't asking the right questions.

One thing bothered my newly calibrated brain, however. "Monty, when was your time machine time displacement system created and started up?"

"Last Thursday."

Chapter 13 - Plans

The next day I tried to think of the necessary things I would need, every detail I could fathom, and all the equipment and systems I might need, and I made a list of the things I thought needed attention for this mission to be accomplished. And so it turned out that a number of things, like a weapon, were going to have be dealt with.

I checked the car's systems and asked Monty questions as necessary. This led me to find out that the car was equipped to fire a few different weapons and to provide targeting and monitoring of all missiles, energy emissions, and the like. But I did not have any ammunition. It was sort of like having a whole rack of rifles in your house without any bullets. Any thoughts of making my own ammunition were quickly ruined by Monty's report of the time necessary to obtain materials and for construction using materials and tools I was unlikely to find. And the weapons we used in military operations here on Earth were incompatible with my car. My system was relatively simple when one considers the source. I had a very sophisticated system by Earth standards.

Now I had to include in my plans a way to either obtain a weapon or make use of the one I had used before. I spent a lot of time considering what my alternatives might be, but I could only think of two real choices. First, I could go and rendezvous with my former self as he hurtled through space on the way to Saturn. This would mean finding him, getting close enough to communicate with him, and convince him to change the plan and fire his missile thirty minutes early. This presented many problems, I thought. I might have to identify myself, and I might have to risk a number of different responses that could make matters worse.

I imagined myself as I had been on Saturday, enjoying the interesting space flight on the way to Dione, enthralled by my new and improved senses and abilities. What if I had been suddenly interrupted by a voice on the communication speakers? How would I have reacted? That would not have been in the schedule, for one thing. And what would I think when the voice failed to identify itself or if it *did* identify itself as myself in the future? I just could not predict what would happen.

The second choice was to meet with Mr. Temm. I could try to explain the whole matter to him, or I could just go ask him for another bomb. He might respond well with either option, but he might not. And there was the further problem of deciding when to visit Mr. Temm. Should it be after my other self was asleep Thursday night or before my other self ever came aboard the big ship? I imagined showing up during the evening so there would be two Demetrius Adriens trying to speak to Mr. Temm and Ravsen at the same time, but that seemed completely out of the question.

I concluded that I could not predict Mr. Temm's reaction either, and I felt as though I had hit a standstill. Was I going to be able to pull this thing off?

"Monty, is it possible for this vehicle to travel to where Mr. Temm is now?" I expected Monty to say, "Yes, but it would take six years," or something, so I quickly added, "I mean, in a short time, such as a day or so?"

But Monty's answer was simple and not so unexpected. "No. This vehicle does not have the capability to jump an interstellar gap."

"Could we give it that capacity?"

"No."

This seemed a bit abrupt, so I pursued the question. "Do you mean we cannot do it at all or that it cannot be done soon enough or that…well, *why* can't we give our ship an interstellar gap-jumping capability?"

"Because the drives and mechanisms and systems are not available in this sector of the galaxy, except in Mr. Temm's vessel, and because this ship is too small, and because it would take forty-seven weeks, and because you could not obtain some of the required data needed to command the operating system without being trained more elaborately.

"And there are other, less significant reasons, which when taken together with the former ones, make the task fundamentally and effectively improbable to be accomplished, if not actually impossible."

I chewed on this for a while. And then I went back in the house and fixed a cup of coffee. I knew I had to keep on trying to figure this out. I felt that I would be able to do this task. I just had to keep on working at it.

After spending the better part of the day doing the chores of life that had been neglected, I sat back with a second cup of coffee. The bills were paid, the calls were answered, the laundry was done, some of the cleaning was accomplished, and I had even made the bed.

I sat down to watch the TV again. It was the first time I had turned it on since hearing the news about Seattle. I wanted to watch an old movie or something, but which one? I read in the television listings that one of Isaac Asimov's robot stories was on one of the movie channels. They had made his science fiction book, *I, Robot*, into a movie. I vaguely remember when this new film came out in the theatres, and I was also reminded of how I had read that book when I was a teenager. Now it was a movie, but I had heard that they had changed the story around so much for the screen adaptation that I never went to see it.

I think it stayed in my mind on that occasion because I now felt like I had Robby the Robot in my garage. His name was Monty, not Robby, but he seemed so much like the robots in Asimov's stories. I remember the trouble those humans in the stories had with various robots who acted unexpectedly, or who had exhibited actual problems or malfunctions. One of the stories was about how a little girl completely burned out a robot's brain just by asking it simple questions. The robot was not able to handle the complexities of even childish thinking.

Monty seemed to be able to answer all of my questions so far.

As I went back out to the garage, I realized I was my own worst enemy. I was too narrow-minded. I didn't ask the right questions. That robot, or computer, probably knew more than anyone on the entire planet, and I just had to ask the right questions.

"Hey, Monty. You got any ideas about how I could go back in time and stop that lizard creature on Dione from firing that weapon a week ago…without any weapons of my own?"

Monty did not answer right away, like he usually did. Perhaps it was my bad grammar. When he spoke, it was slowly, as if he had not understood the question but was determined to answer it anyway the best he could.

"The creature did not fire the weapon, Demetrius. Would you like to ask another question?"

Maybe this robot was having a malfunction of his own, but I was hopeful again as new ideas came into my mind. "Well, maybe he didn't intentionally fire it, but while the weapon was still under construction, it let off a burst of energy. Surely you remember that. Anyway, how do you think we could prevent that burst from having happened?"

"We could go back to a time before the energy burst on Dione, and you could disable the weapon and then leave before the bomb the other Demetrius Adrien fired from his Camry destroyed the area."

I wondered why I had not thought of this myself.

"Is that plan likely to succeed? Isn't there some risk that the creature would prevent me from getting anywhere near the area? Surely we could not go in so close and remain undetected, could we?"

"There would be risk. Without a weapon to fire from a distance, however, I see no other way to prevent the blast from occurring without risking death or unpredictable bodily consequence to you."

"Monty, do you know why or how that blast was fired, even though it was not supposed to have been possible?"

"I have a theory that may explain why, but I cannot prove it without more data. The Elixir electro-proton weapon has a system of storing energy to be used at a later time. Though your planet's technology has not discovered the phase of matter and energy called Elixir, you have been made aware of this technology in your training. The Elixir power continuum is contained in a vessel that must be fully discharged when the weapon is disassembled. However, this creature may not have fully discharged the continuum. I suspect that this would be an irresponsible act to the intelligent race capable of inventing such a weapon, but the creature on Dione was not of that race.

"I believe the power left in the Elixir continuum vessel may have erupted from the weapon, perhaps as a surprise to the creature who may have been in the act of programming the targeting system."

This seemed perfectly logical to me. The beast probably was not a very self-disciplined sort. I could imagine that. "Do you have a record of the exact moment when that blast erupted?"

"Yes, Mr. Adrien."

I already assumed that the computer's memory would have the exact time of the blast. Imagine my surprise when Monty spoke to me, without my asking him anything.

"Demetrius, could I ask you something?"

"Sure, Monty. What's up?"

"I have readings of the blast the creature's weapon fired accidentally, and I saw its trajectory toward Earth. Do you know what it hit?"

Chapter 14 – Monty's Problem

I believed that Monty knew everything that happened on planet Earth up until the moment I locked him in the garage. So it was a surprise to me that he didn't know about the strange phenomenon in Seattle. But he didn't know. He had not heard about my family being killed. He was not keeping up with the news. I wanted to take care of something right away before I answered his question. I wasn't sure if I wanted to answer his question at all, to tell you the truth.

"Monty, are you able to monitor the radio waves all around us and learn of news around the world?"

"Yes."

"Why have you not been doing so?"

"Because you have not commanded me to do so."

"Oh."

This was an answer I wouldn't have expected from another person, but Monty was, well, you know.

"Monty, I want you to understand something. I do not know the extent of your knowledge, your database, or whatever you call it – your memory. I do not know what you are capable of and I do not know what questions to ask you, even when I have a need for information." For some reason I was getting emotional, perhaps even angry. I just knew that was how I wanted to feel right then, and it felt good.

"I wish you would just take care of whatever you are here to take care of and don't wait for me to tell you. I suppose you won't recharge your batteries if I don't command it, so you'll run out of power and die, and I'll never know it. Just monitor the airwaves and learn all you can. And if there is any reason – I mean even the remotest reason you can conceive of why I might need to know something, just tell me. But be reasonable."

I was quiet for a minute. There were probably some other things I needed to tell Monty to do or not to do, but I was finished for the moment. I needed to answer his question. So, after I breathed for a minute, I told him.

"The blast from that Elixir electro-proton gun hit the planet Earth in Seattle, Washington, and killed nineteen people. Three of those people were my own wife and children." There, now he knew. And I was reminded.

Monty did not answer, and he did not ask any more questions for a while.

I was back in the house packing my Taekwon-Do uniform into my gear bag, getting ready to go to class. I was startled to hear Monty's voice. I was upstairs in the room farthest away from the garage. "Mr. Adrien? Can you hear me?"

The sound was coming from my wristwatch. I guess Mr. Temm had not just cleaned it, but he had modified it as well, or maybe replaced it.

"What's up, Monty? I can hear you fine."

"I know I cannot tell you everything you would remotely be interested to know, as you instructed me, but I believe I can indeed carry out your command, nevertheless. I will give you important information as needed in balance with the amount of knowledge you would otherwise receive as a resident of Earth without my help. This is an equation I can obey."

"Great. Do you have some information for me now?"

"Yes. I wanted you to know that your wristwatch has some new functions available to you now, from your database from Mr. Temm, one of which is the function of a communication link with your car's computer. That is, me. I will be able to tell with a very high accuracy if you are alone so that other people do not hear my voice. If you are not in a position to listen to me audibly, the display on the watch will act as a screen for text or video. And, as an added feature, the watch will vibrate slightly when there is a need for me to communicate with you in secret."

Monty sounded like a commercial. I was smiling broadly as I listened to him, carrying my gear bag downstairs to the garage. I did notice, now that he had said something about it, that it was easy to remember the necessary instructions to operate the new wristwatch. I stepped into the garage and continued the conversation with Monty in person.

"Are there any other new items Mr. Temm gave me that I have not made use of yet?"

"Possibly. I am not aware of everything you have done since you acquired them. Perhaps you knew that the remote control you use to open the garage door also does a number of other functions. These are suited for purposes you will most likely need while traveling. I recommend that you leave it with the car, but that is not required. Your cell phone also has a few added features that you may not have used yet, mostly related to communications. And you have already seen the laptop computer presently docked to the desktop computer in your home, which will allow you to have access to all of my functions when the car itself is not with you. Just take the laptop along any time you need me, and my assistance will be conveniently available when you are not traveling in this vehicle.

"If ever there is a feature I believe you might benefit from and if it appears that you may have forgotten about it, then I will let you know if it is convenient to do so at the time."

"Thanks, Monty."

We were now driving to the Taekwon-Do school, which was only about ten minutes away. About halfway there, Monty spoke to me.

"Demetrius."

"Yes, Monty."

"I have not told you one thing. Perhaps I should do so now."

"What is it?" I didn't know if this was going to be a surprise or just computer trivia, but my ears perked up. Monty's unsolicited statements and questions were infrequent but usually significant.

"My purpose for existing is to take care of you."

I remained silent as I considered this. I had alluded to Monty's purpose once before, when I had become frustrated and overwhelmed with all his lack of initiative. I had said, "I wish you would just take care of whatever you are here to take care of and don't wait for me to tell you." Now he was informing me that he did have a reason for acting the way he was. He was trying to figure me out.

I supposed I wasn't making it easy for him. The significance of this was not lost, however. I realized that this was one of Mr. Temm's gifts. He had given me a slave, a servant who existed solely for the purpose of serving and protecting only me. Monty wanted to please me. I thought he might find pleasing me a real problem, at least he would have if he were human. But I figured the job would suit him as long as we could get used to each other. It looked like he was making progress already, come to think of it.

The Black Belt test was rescheduled for two more weeks on a Saturday. I never knew the trouble it had been to change Master Titus's travel plans, but it must have cost somebody something. He lived in Missouri, and his schedule was rather busy. But when Mr. Halyard lost three students to a fatal accident, well, I guess it was understandable to interrupt schedules.

I had a plan to change the schedule again, but no one would notice. I figured when I went back in time and stopped that weapon from erupting its blast of deadly energy, then Seattle would be saved along with the rest of the planet, and we would never have to reschedule anything. My wife and kids would fly home as expected, and we would have our Black Belt test when we were supposed to have had it.

Of course, I hadn't worked out the details yet. I had decided to fly out to a place between the orbits of Mars and Jupiter to rendezvous with my former self and speed up so we could blow up that alien at least thirty minutes earlier. I thought this was at least more predictable than trying to discuss the matter with Mr. Temm. I knew that Mr. Temm had learned something about the concept of urgency and the need to act quickly. But he had led a slow life with not a care in the world for thousands of years, right? No, it would be much better to speak to an earthling about an urgent change of plans.

And I could trust the driver of that Camry to make the right choice. After all, I could trust myself, couldn't I?

I wish I had had the time and opportunity to learn more about time travel. Maybe I should have run some experiments to see how it would be to talk to myself, only in a controlled setting of some sort. But here I was at Taekwon-Do. I would think about it later.

Classes went well. It was good to be back. After I helped teach some Yellow Tabs working on their first pattern, *Chon-ji*, in the first class, and I helped the Green Tabs learn the rest of their new self-defense techniques in the second class, I was ready for the adult class. And though we had some lower belt ranks, we got to do all the patterns we had time for. After the opening stretching exercises, we went straight into patterns, and I again felt like I could do no wrong. I tried to stay relaxed, wondering if Mr. Halyard had noticed any change in my performance. He had said nothing yet.

But, it hadn't been very long since I had been back with my new and improved physiology. Perhaps he hadn't really had time to notice me yet. Regardless of these thoughts, I stayed alert and busy during class with little time for distraction.

After class, as I was about to leave, Mr. Halyard said something I overheard. He was talking with the two Black Belts who always seemed to stay after everyone was gone. He was telling them that we were expecting a visitor from Kentucky. I didn't want to be rude and listen in on someone else's conversation, but I did catch the information that this visitor had his own Taekwon-Do school and might bring a couple of students with him. As I left, I wondered if the visitor was going to be here for my test and whether the new schedule change I had in mind would affect this visitor's schedule. We'll see. Visitors were infrequent, and this one was probably not any big deal. I liked meeting new people as much as anyone, but right now I was sort of busy.

I needed to get on with my mission to Saturn as soon as possible. I was getting impatient. But I was reluctant to just hop in the car and tell Monty to take me back to last Saturday and start looking for a blue Toyota flying from the moon to Saturn.

We shouldn't actually have any problem finding my former self. The tracking of another ship was really only hindered when the ship was trying not to be tracked. But I remember when I was traveling to Dione, I was not suspecting anyone to be following me. Back then, I had known I was the only one with a ship like this in the whole solar system. Well, that was going to change, because I was going back. There would be two of us.

"Monty, I want to take a trip tonight back to the time and place where that alien's Elixir weapon erupted its energy blast toward Earth. Are you able to take me there and then tonight?"

"Sure, Demetrius. All I ask is that you allow me to get out of sight before we do any flying, which would appear abnormal to the Earth people. Once we are away, you can either tell me precisely where and when you wish to go or you can pilot the ship yourself if you so choose."

I was getting a little bit nervous about this whole thing already, but I said, "How about I let you control the time travel, and I will fly the space dimensions?"

"Okay"

"I want to go back to Sunday morning, when we were just finished passing the orbit of Jupiter and looking to Saturn, say about eight o'clock. Can you handle the timing of the speed for space travel with our arrival near the Camry at that time?" It sounded amazingly complicated to me. Was I going to fly from Earth to Saturn for all those hours? Something occurred to me. Could I also include some of that faster traveling Mr. Temm had employed when he took me from the parking garage on Earth to the moon in an instant? That kind of traveling would save all those hours required to get up to speed and slow back down again.

I asked Monty about Mr. Temm's transporter. Did we have any of that technology with us? But Monty said no. Actually Mr. Temm had snatched me from Earth with a cargo mover. He had often benefited from moving cargo a small gap in time as well as space. I could only imagine how that would work. It didn't seem very important for Mr. Temm to ever need to save time.

"When you were brought to the Friendland ship, you did not need to be moved in time. But when Mr. Temm returned you to Earth, he moved us both in time so you would not have inconvenience with your surroundings. This had been planned before you were even selected as the individual person to help the Friendlanders. My time displacement system was initiated earlier that day, before I was even placed in your vehicle, when the plans for your mission were being organized."

Chapter 15 - The Board

I was ready this time. I even packed a lunch.

I might have left for Saturn right away, but I got a call from my Taekwon-Do instructor, Mr. Halyard. He asked me if I would be available again to help teach classes on Saturday. I had the distinct impression that this was not the reason he had called. There was something in his voice, a slight hesitation, as if perhaps he wasn't sure if he should go ahead and bring up the real subject on his mind. Maybe it was just my imagination.

After I told him I would be glad to teach classes on Saturday, he asked me if I would be there tonight for class. It was Thursday again, so I told him yes, even though I was very interested in starting out on my mission. He asked if I would be able to stop by his office after the last class tonight, because he had something to talk with me about. I said, "Yes, sir. No problem." What choice did I have? And, besides, I was interested in why he might want to talk to me after class. Of course, I would be there. No problem.

Actually, this call from Mr. Halyard was so unusual that I put off the mission until after class and this mysterious meeting. I figured I had a time machine, what did it matter if I waited a few more hours to travel back to a specific time in the past? Mr. Halyard had made me curious.

As I drove to the training center, known as the *do jang*, I was a little relieved to be postponing my second big trip to Saturn. I focused my thoughts on Taekwon-Do for the time being and set myself to be patient. I wanted to know why Mr. Halyard needed to speak to me. I hoped it wasn't going to be bad news, or some surprise. But, oh, well, I had to be patient.

The classes were pretty much the same as always, with never a dull moment as Mr. Halyard gave the students new ways to think about the drills and exercises they were doing, new ways to perform the same basic fundamentals, and new applications for old ideas. I did my part teaching the groups of colored belt students. I always found the adult students so much easier to work with. They could understand my conversation. With kids, well, I just had to be patient with them and try to make them do something like the real thing. I had to remind myself that these kids' parents were paying for their kids to be here, and Mr. Halyard needed them to be happy.

I don't know if he needed me to be happy, however. I was paying my monthly dues, like everyone else, and sometimes the funds had been hard to come by. It had always been a family of four, and that meant four times the monthly fee. I supposed I was a good student. I had always tried to be. But I never had anybody thanking me for any of this. I had never expected thanks. It was just me doing what I was told and what was expected. A student always said, "Yes, sir," to his instructor and did whatever he was told.

I had a good workout, but we did mostly patterns and some sparring drills with partners. In our school, we didn't actually fight with each other while wearing our sparring gear nearly as much as you might think. I imagined the reason was because I was told you don't really learn to fight by fighting, but by studying fighting. We did drills and patterns to learn how to move right, and that was going to make us good fighters, so they said.

After classes were over, I hung around waiting for Mr. Halyard to become available for our meeting. It seemed like he always had students and parents of students standing in line to speak to him after class. I had never stuck around much after classes; we always wanted to get home and have dinner, and the evening was late for family people like us who always had to get up early the next day. But tonight I was alone. And I had not woke up very early for a week or so.

The three Black Belts who had been assisting with the classes along with me tonight were the last ones to leave, as usual. One of them eventually left, but the other two did something that surprised me. One of them spoke to me. "Are you going to stick around and help us tonight, sir?"

He was smiling and cheerful, but I really didn't know what he was talking about. I explained, "No, sir. I have a meeting with Mr. Halyard tonight. In his office."

This young man's name was Stockman. We called him Mr. Stockman, even though he was only about seventeen years old. As a Black Belt, however, he was our instructor, and we were not supposed to use his first name. He had called me "sir" as well, but that was only because I was older than he was. Mr. Stockman was always polite and respectful. He was a good student, I suppose. My red colored belt was too much in my mind as I spoke with Mr. Stockman. It seemed somehow backwards for the younger student to outrank the older one.

But none of this is what surprised me.

The surprise was when Mr. Stockman opened up the supply closet and got out a big vacuum cleaner, like one of those Shop-Vacs used in garages. He took it out on the *do jang* floor and proceeded to systematically vacuum the padded floor, one square at a time. The floor was made up of interlocking squares about a yard in size. It looked like Mr. Stockman was determined to vacuum every single square inch of that floor. And it looked like this was not the first time he had done it.

The other Black Belt, also about seventeen or eighteen years old, was busy wiping chairs, walls, and surfaces all over the training center. He had a container of cleansing wipes, and he seemed just as determined to wipe every square inch he could reach. He was headed toward the men's room with a fresh supply of wipes when Mr. Halyard called me over.

He had been on the phone, and was finally available for our meeting. He waved me over to his office, which was really not much of an office, but a small room set off from the waiting area where he could keep his computer and files and such. He asked me to have a seat. He looked cheerful, as if everything was better than normal in his life.

"Mr. Adrien, I want you to know again that we are all deeply sorrowful about losing your family, and we know it must be difficult for you. Thanks for helping out in class tonight. I'm glad you're back. I wouldn't blame you if you stayed away longer or took some time off. But I am glad you're back. How was your workout tonight?"

I knew this chitchat was out of politeness, and that was okay. I would have acted the same way, I suppose, if the roles were switched. But I knew he had something else he was going to speak to me about.

Mr. Halyard was about eight years younger than me, but he was a Fourth Degree Black Belt. His uniform had black stripes down each arm and leg. We students with the various colored belts all just had solid white uniforms, and the lower ranked Black Belts had some black trim along the bottom edges of their jacket, but Mr. Halyard's was the really cool uniform. He had been doing Taekwon-Do ever since he was twelve years old.

I answered his question, "It felt good. I think a good Taekwon-Do workout is like therapy in more ways than one." He was silent long enough for me to ask, "Could I ask you a question, sir?"

"Sure," he said.

"How often do those guys clean up this place? I always assumed you had a cleaning service come in here in the daytime."

"Ha ha! No, we do all the cleaning ourselves every night after class. If there are no helpers on any given night, I do it myself. It's not too bad. I get home before midnight, and I don't have to get up early the next day."

This was rather surprising to me, but it made sense. After all, he was running a business here and needed to save on expenses like anyone else. "Maybe you could get the lower ranks to do the cleaning. I would think once you become a Black Belt, you might not have to do that kind of thing anymore." I was trying to be as cheerful as everyone else was being tonight, but I wasn't quite sure if I was pulling it off.

He said, "Oh, I don't make Mr. Stockman and Mr. Davis do the cleaning. They volunteer their time." Mr. Halyard got up from his chair and went to a bookshelf, looking for a volume as he spoke. He returned and opened up one of the many volumes of the Taekwon-Do encyclopedia and showed me a picture.

He said, "This is in a section about public service. A Taekwon-Do student should give of his time to benefit the community around him with other services besides just teaching Taekwon-Do." The picture showed a bunch of students in Taekwon-Do uniforms sweeping the sidewalks in what looked like a public park area. I noticed the black stripes on the arms and legs of their uniforms. They were Fourth Degree Black Belts sweeping the sidewalks with their uniforms on. Interesting.

We were in the office with the door shut, but we could see the workout floor through a glass window. Mr. Stockman was still vacuuming each square in order, row after row. Mr. Davis was probably cleaning the restrooms or taking out the trash. They did this every night?

Mr. Halyard didn't say anything as he returned the volume to the shelf. As he sat down again, I asked, "Did you want to speak to me about something, Mr. Halyard?"

"Yes. I wanted to try to talk you into not quitting Taekwon-Do when you get your Black Belt."

This was a shock. I had never said anything about quitting to anyone, even my own wife. The shock, however, was really not about that. The shock was because it was true, and Mr. Halyard had no business reading my mind. I almost became angry as I answered. "Sir, I had no intention of quitting," and I made some incoherent sounds of protest as I sat back and sighed.

He continued politely, "Just in case you were thinking about it. I also wanted to tell you about something I probably should have told you before. Do you remember when you tested for Blue Tab?"

This seemed like a strange thing to talk about, but, of course, I could remember it very well. Getting the blue tabs on his green belt was a big deal for a Taekwon-Do student because it was halfway on the road to Black Belt. The Blue Tabs were considered senior ranks, having made it to Fifth Gup. "Yes. I remember."

"You may remember you had to break a board with a jump high front snap kick, and it took you about five attempts to do it. The board was very tough, and it was probably unfair to you that it didn't break on the first attempt. Mr. Stockman was holding that board, and he had to stretch to get it high enough for you. Do you remember what happened?"

"Yes, sir. I got stubborn and determined to break that board, and I finally got it."

"Mr. Stockman says he watched your face. He said you looked confused at first about why the board wasn't breaking. And then he knew you were going to break that board on the next try. He saw it in your eyes."

I decided to let Mr. Halyard tell the story without my interruption. I did not know why he was recounting this episode. At the time of the event he was referring to, I had actually been embarrassed by the whole thing. I had felt that the audience must be ashamed to see a grown man who couldn't even break one board.

"Remember what happened? You jumped higher than you ever had, you kicked harder than you ever had, and Mr. Stockman was left holding two pieces of wood, unaware that a third piece was flying over his head. You broke the center right out of that gnarly board."

"I remember."

"I want you to know something that happened you were unaware of. In the audience was a man with his son. The kid was about seven years old. His dad was amazed that his son was so intent on watching you, Mr. Adrien. That seven-year-old kid watched you very closely. He never took his eyes off of you. And when you broke that board, little Isaac broke out in applause and cheered. Isaac's dad had tears in his eyes. And Isaac became a Taekwon-Do student two days later."

There was a minute or so of silence as I just looked at my knees. Mr. Halyard said, "That sort of thing happens all the time. You have no idea how many people you are influencing, especially when you are testing or doing a demonstration or teaching.

"That's why I want you to reconsider quitting. You have a great future here if you stay. And it will help my school to have you here."

I told him, "Well, sir, I hadn't planned on quitting, but I appreciate your concern. And thanks for the feedback. It's good to know somebody noticed me somewhere along the way. Is there anything else, sir?"

"One thing. I wanted to check if the schedule for your Black Belt test was okay for you, if you have errands or business to attend to. I wanted to make sure you feel up to it with all that has happened recently. Everyone would understand if you wanted to wait longer."

"I'll be fine, sir. In two weeks, I should be even better. I hope to be back to normal as soon as possible." I realized as I finished that this might sound a bit funny. I was perhaps not acting like a man who just suffered the tragic loss of three family members. I had a different plan in mind and a different hope.

As I opened the office door to leave, Mr. Halyard spoke again, "There is one more thing I wanted to mention." I closed the door again, but I remained standing.

"When you become a Black Belt, you won't have to pay the monthly fee anymore, and you can still train in the senior classes. But I will use you as an instructor whenever you are here, and you may find yourself wanting to find your own time to train outside of class. The facility is available to you any time I am here. Someday maybe I can get you a key to the front door, but right now I'm the only one who has one.

"Thanks for your help tonight. See you Saturday."

Chapter 16 - The Mission, Again

Like I said, I was ready this time. I even packed a lunch.

Believe it or not, as we were taking off for Saturn, I thought of an alternative idea for how to destroy that creature on Dione earlier, before the Elixir energy blast erupted from his weapon. It was a little late, but I asked Monty about it.

"Hey, Monty." I had along the way somewhere become careful never to surprise Monty, for some reason. I always found myself speaking carefully when presenting new ideas to him.

"Yes, Demetrius?" Considering that we were already traveling about three hundred million miles per hour, Monty's voice was as calm and melodious as ever.

"Could you fly this car without me in it?"

"Nope."

That was easy. I had had this idea to send Monty by himself back to last Sunday on Dione and let him take care of things without me. But it looked like that was going to be impossible. I asked him why he couldn't fly the ship without me in it.

"Because it was made for you to fly. My abilities do not include certain things that need to be done, mostly decision-making, while flying a vehicle. I also think it has something to do with my role in your life. Mr. Chamm would not have wanted me to fly without a pilot, and I think he would not approve of you sending me off alone. I believe I am not capable of getting out of some of the possible situations that could arise if I were without a pilot, so he made it impossible for me to run the ship without you in it."

"Could you fly it with a different pilot? Someone else besides me?"

"No way. No one can even start up this vehicle except you, Demetri." He sounded cheerful as he said it. I decided to drop the subject.

Well, I don't want you to be disappointed, so I'll tell you in advance that I never did have that conversation with my past self to convince him to speed things up and launch the missile thirty minutes earlier. Sorry, but I'll explain why not, as we continue.

However, I don't think you will be disappointed when you find out what actually did happen. As it turns out, the actual course of events was more difficult, more dangerous, and more intense than I expected, and I would surely not have done it this way if I had thought of it beforehand. Here's what happened.

I had every intention of swinging close to the Camry from last Sunday and communicating with that version of me driving it. Monty had done his magic and taken us back in time, but I never knew exactly at what point the time travel happened. To me, we just flew to Saturn. But when we got there, it was last Sunday, again.

We were actually quite some distance away, with about an hour until that evil blast would erupt from the creature's weapon. I was able to see the Camry on my sensor screen, and Monty confirmed that we had found it. The sky was filled with Saturn as we flew along. The speed was incredible, but you couldn't tell unless some slow-moving object was close by. And as we approached Saturn it seemed like there were plenty of slow-moving objects. Saturn has so many moons that it seemed there were heavenly objects everywhere, all going in haphazard directions. They weren't, but our relative speed made it seem so.

"Okay, Monty, I want to open a channel to the Camry on the communication system." This was just casual conversation on my part, and I thought I was doing what we had planned all along. But Monty did not open any channels. "Monty? Are you okay?"

"I'm fine, Demetrius. Why do you ask?"

"I requested that you open a communication channel so I can call the Camry and talk to, er, the other Demetrius. But you didn't do it. Are you all right with that, or what?"

"Sorry, Mr. Adrien. You cannot talk to the other Demetrius."

"Why not?"

"That would be illegal."

"What the heck do I care if it's illegal? Just do it!"

My wife often told our friends that if I ever said the word "heck," that I was really getting mad. That was about as bad as my language ever got. She said if I ever dared to say "darn it," someone was really in trouble. Well, this was one of those "darn it" times. After all that discussion and apparently wasted time with Monty, now he was not going to let me talk to the past me in the Camry we were now following on the occasion of last Sunday near the planet Saturn. I was about to get furious. And who had legal jurisdiction for time travel infractions? I was going to have to get an explanation later.

"Monty, how am I going to stop that energy blast from hitting Seattle if I can't talk to the guy with the missile and make him blow up that weapon before it fires?"

"Oh, we can stop the energy blast. That won't be happening for forty-three more minutes."

"What? I thought we were going to blow up the creature thirty minutes early? Now you're telling me there's another way to stop the energy blast?"

"Sure. You did not tell me that our top priority was to stop the energy blast. You wanted me to take you here to this time, so here we are at this time." His cheerful voice was very annoying right then. I had to calm down. There was apparently still hope.

"Monty. How are we going to stop that energy blast from hitting Seattle?"

"There are a couple of things to decide, Demetrius. Would you like to deflect the energy blast so it misses the Earth entirely, or would you like to try to hit something else besides Seattle?"

"I want it to miss the Earth entirely! I thought you knew that, for crying out loud! What are we waiting for?"

"We are waiting for the blast to be fired. We cannot deflect it until after that happens." I was in a sort of panic, but I began to realize that panic was not very smart. I needed to get ahold of myself. Monty's ludicrous logic was actually quite effective for releasing some tension. I laughed. Yes, I laughed out loud. I couldn't believe this was happening. Calm down, calm down.

Okay, we were going to wait for the blast to come blazing out of that weapon at the speed of light and then deflect it. Great. Monty knew how to do it. I needed to trust him. "Monty, even though we know the exact moment the energy blast will be fired, don't we need to do something to, like, get ready?"

"I recommend that you fly into the path of the Elixir energy blast so that it is deflected toward the Sun. It would do no harm to the Sun. And, in addition, the blast would be stopped when it strikes the Sun, and it could not go past and strike Venus or another unfortunate planet elsewhere in the galaxy. That would be unlikely, of course."

"Monty. This is serious, are you joking? Monty, this may come as a surprise to you, but I do not have the ability to fly this ship with the precision you are suggesting. Can you please navigate the ship to deflect the energy blast into the Sun?"

"Yes, I can. Would you like me to turn toward the best trajectory I can calculate for such a feat?"

"Yes! Please do! Thanks, Monty. That would mean a lot to me." I could tell Monty and I needed to continue working on our communication skills.

After about thirty minutes of nail-biting anticipation, it occurred to me that I needed to ask Monty an important question. "Excuse me, Monty?"

"Yes. Demetrius."

"There wouldn't, by any chance, be any danger when we deflect this Elixir energy blast, would there? You made it sound like we were going to run into it with the car and sort of push it off course. Is that likely to harm us in any way?" I was afraid maybe Monty now believed that I was willing to die to save the planet Earth or even Seattle.

"Heck, no Demetrius! I am going to use the GAC, or Gravitonic Acceleration Compensator, to push the energy blast away a bit. The angle doesn't need to be much. The Sun may seem big to you, but hitting it squarely from this distance is going to take some precision."

I think Monty was playing a game. He wanted to see if he could hit the exact center of the Sun with that Elixir blast. I don't know if he was actually concentrating or what, but I decided not to speak to him while the time approached. I would hate to interrupt him in the middle of his golf swing, so to speak.

The blast was, of course, precisely on time. It came shooting out of Dione just when we knew it would, and it headed straight for us. Monty had turned the ship to race back toward Earth, and I think we were, for a while, traveling as fast as the ship could go, accelerating to almost the speed of light.

It was a special effects marvel when I could see the energy blast in the rearview mirror. It was quite scary. I turned in the seat to watch the great purple blast of lightning through the back window, but this was not a thin line of electricity. Imagine if lightning were about eighty feet wide and about a thousand feet long, and you get the idea. And there was a strange and eerie look about it as it shimmered and pulsated as it sped through the heavens. The Elixir blast and the Camry were traveling together, so it appeared that the purple pulsating lightning was catching up to us slowly. I could scarcely imagine what this scene might have looked like to a passing ship. I suppose some alien may have watched with binoculars as we hurtled past at breakneck speed, like a rushing motorist being chased by an alien force of purple lightning.

As the monstrous blob of energy caught up to us, the sky was filled with the purple, weird lightning, but Monty said nothing. And I was not breathing properly. This was intense! I knew that the glass in my windows was dark like a welder's mask because otherwise the light or heat or radiation would have blinded or burned or killed me. But even with that, I was squinting with impatience. I wished we could hurry up and get away from this thing. And then, Monty made a noise which must have been a laugh.

At the same time, we moved off to one side and slowed down. I didn't feel the motion because the GAC did its job of protecting the vehicle's passenger, me, but the energy blast seemed to move away from us and speed off to parts unknown. Monty said, "That was cool, wasn't it Demetrius?"

"Yeah, Monty, real cool." I was breathing hard and sweating. Maybe this whole business was finally over. I was afraid to know what had happened. Had it worked? Why had Monty laughed? Was he going loony on me?"

I knew it would be an hour or so before the blast hit the Sun or whatever it was going to hit. We just needed to go back and wait. But then something hit me.

I realized I couldn't go back to the Earth and just go home now. We had been traveling for many hours, but it was Sunday again - the same Sunday I had heard the news about Seattle. I would be getting the phone call in a few hours. There would be a funeral coming up. Wait!

There wasn't going to be a funeral! Seattle would have no "meteorite" hitting it now. I had to think. Back when I was sitting on the couch, the news came on the television. I was falling asleep, and the news about Seattle woke me. Now that news was not going to wake me. My whole week would be totally different. I would not have any need to plan the week I actually planned. I had to get back to the house.

"Monty, where are we going?"

"We are on a course for the Earth, but at a more reasonable pace. Where would you like to go?"

"I would like to go home. But I think one of my former selves is there in the house right now. And there would be another Camry in the garage, I suppose. What are my legal alternatives for going back to my house?"

"Good question. Shall we go find out?"

I dozed off and slept some on the trip back, but I remember being slightly tumbled out of a dream with the sound of Monty saying something, then I went off back to sleep again. I vaguely remember him saying, "Bull's-eye!"

Chapter 17 - Let's Talk

I had to assume that Monty wouldn't know if he would be able to take us to my house until he tried to do so, and we didn't discuss the matter while we traveled. I had too much thinking to do, and my mind was swimming in possibilities. But I needn't have troubled myself. If I had known the right questions, Monty would have solved our problem immediately. Right?

I needed to teach him how to solve problems without waiting for me to ask the right questions. Well, life is full of funny troubles. I almost laughed as I realized the unique situation I was in compared to all the other people on Earth.

I also was almost afraid to hope that I was actually going to see my wife and kids again. It was difficult to imagine how this was all going to turn out.

We approached the house, now traveling like an ordinary car on the street. I felt like a stranger to my own neighborhood. Could it really be last Monday, again? When we got to the corner where I would normally turn into my subdivision, Monty said, "Sorry, Mr. Adrien, I can't let you drive any closer to the house."

"Why not? Is *that* illegal too? How are you making this decision?"

"It is part of my programming. Apparently I understand the laws of time travel only at the very time when it matters. I simply cannot go any closer." The car drove straight instead of slowing down to turn. I had a distinct memory of the time the car had turned by itself into that parking lot last Thursday.

"I believe, Demetrius, that Mr. Temm and Mr. Chamm have made the time displacement system operate this way for your protection."

Well, that was certainly probable. All the thoughts I had imagined while we traveled back from Saturn had certainly suggested that it would be dangerous to walk into my house and surprise the Demetrius who would be there doing the laundry or something. If I couldn't go home, where could I go? Maybe I should get a hotel room and wait for this to all blow over.

But it occurred to me that it might not all blow over so easily. The Demetrius Adrien in my house right now was not about to travel back in time to try to blow up an alien creature for the second time. But he had to. Otherwise, how could I actually be here right now?

We were just driving around the district, as Monty awaited orders and I just thought about things. I looked for a place to park the car so I could talk to Monty. There was no need to drive around.

I didn't really know that I had an actual problem to solve until I started telling Monty about the situation. But as I told him about it, it became more and more clear to me that I had a serious problem. And while I was realizing that I had a problem, I also knew, pretty much, how it had to be solved. But I was trying not to think about that. Surely there would be a simpler way if I considered all the possibilities. But here's how the conversation went.

"Monty, I think I might need your help on something."

"What is it, Mr. Adrien? I'll do my best to understand, and I'll help you ask the right questions if I can."

"There is a man named Demetrius Adrien in my house right now. He did not get any news that Seattle was struck by a meteor or anything like that. There was no such news on the TV today. He probably slept well and called his wife without ever a thought. And now he plans to go to the airport on Wednesday to pick up that wife and the two children. He is going to bring them home, and she will be tired and probably go to bed early." And *he* will go to bed with her. "And then, Monty, he is going to test for his Black Belt on Saturday." *My* Black Belt.

"In the meantime, I will be here in a parking lot making sure he doesn't know I exist. Therefore, I cannot use his bank account. I cannot visit his friends. I cannot ever go to Taekwon-Do class again in this city." Not anywhere. It wouldn't even help if I traveled back to the future where I came from. He would still be living without a care in the world with my wife, spending my money.

This was when I realized what I had to do. It was a tremendous and insane shock. After about ninety seconds, I said, "Monty, there is also another Monty in his garage." *My* garage.

"I think you would agree with me that this is not a very good situation."

"Yes, Demetrius, I do agree, now that you mention it."

"If I were to walk up to my house tonight while Demetrius was sleeping, what would you do Monty?"

"I think you need to be concerned with the other Monty more than with me, sir. I have no problem just waiting here for you, now that you've explained the way things are."

"What do you think the other Monty would do if I walked up to the house?"

"That is a difficult question. His programming prevents him from doing anything to cause problems. However, I believe he would not interfere."

"What would you do if a second Demetrius Adrien walked up to us right now?"

"I am not sure if I can know for certain, but I suspect that I would just consider him to be you. And I would simply try to take care of him according to my programming. I think my programming and purpose would apply to both of you."

"Monty, we cannot live in secret while that other Demetrius is living out the rest of his life with my wife and my bank account. I have to eliminate him somehow. But I need your help. I need a weapon. Is there anything at all that I am perhaps forgetting that could be used as a weapon against the other Demetrius?"

I expected this to either cause a problem for Monty or to simply get a no for an answer. But Monty came through.

"Your cell phone has a useful feature."

Of course, the EMC. I recalled now that the instructions for the cell phone features were all in my training database, and I immediately remembered that the Emergency Matter Converter, or EMC, was to be used only on rocks and dust and never on living creatures. But it could certainly be used on a human as a weapon. The creators of this feature were not warriors. They did not even dream that the EMC feature would ever be purposefully used this way.

The EMC was for the purpose of getting energy. If you ever needed help when your spacecraft broke down or ran out of fuel, you could point your EMC at a rock and convert the rock's mass into pure energy. This would then be absorbed into the mini-continuum pack in the phone. You would then have spare energy to charge up anything you needed.

If I pointed it at Demetrius Adrien…

That was a bit scary.

"Monty. I am going to go to the house and visit Mr. Adrien. Can you tell me what he is doing right now?"

"He is asleep. It is now 12:37 A.M. on Tuesday."

"I have another thing I need to do. If I were to bring the other Camry back here, what would you do?"

"I think it is probable that I would leave here when you came within approximately a half mile of this location."

"I was afraid of that. I suppose you know that we need to destroy that other Camry as well as the other Demetrius. Can you help me do that?"

"I have already considered that. I have an idea for the solution to that problem. I believe the best thing would be for you to keep the other Monty and destroy me."

This was a jolt. I was hoping maybe the EMC would work on something as big as the Camry, and there would be no problem. "Monty, why should I destroy *you* instead of the other one?"

"Mr. Adrien, the Monty that is in your garage right now has a complete defensive system to hinder accidental or intentional matter conversion as well as strikes from any and every weapon known to your planet. He will not be harmed by your EMC."

I knew that. I just had forgotten. Of course I could not destroy a ship made to withstand even the intense energy of that Elixir blast. The other Monty would surely defend himself.

"But, Monty, how am I going to destroy you? Will you simply sit there and let me shoot you with my EMC?"

"No, the car's defensive system is automatic. I cannot turn it off. The EMC would have no effect on this craft either. However, it would be easy for me to destroy this vehicle myself. I could crash into the Sun at full speed. I will try to hit the bull's-eye to maximize the certainty of destruction. You can tell the other Monty about our adventure someday if you wish. He will especially like the part about the Elixir energy blast following us so close. That was very cool!"

This was a very interesting theory. I was suddenly aware how much this talking computer had learned about life. Maybe there was hope for him yet. He had apparently learned how to fly without a pilot, too.

"Hey, Monty, I need you to wait here for me to return. I want to, um, give you something."

"Sure, Mr. Adrien. I'll be here. Before you leave, sir. Could I ask you a question?"

"Sure, Monty, what's up?"

"Are you planning to commit suicide or homicide?"

I almost choked, but I managed to hold it in. After I recovered, during a dramatic pause, I said, "Monty, there's hope for you yet. You're developing a sense of humor."

I walked to the house, and although it was less than a mile, it was one of the longest walks I ever took. I wanted all this to just be over with. Maybe I could try to learn *Kwan-gae* pattern from memory and not think about what I was doing or where I was going. I knew I was not supposed to do it. That was a Black Belt pattern, and I wasn't a Black Belt yet. But I wasn't so sure the rules applied to me. Let's see, it started out in a parallel ready stance with the hands together over the head, and it looked like the first two movements took you slowly to a new ready stance with the hands down lower. And then you stepped out slowly with the left foot.

But the idea that there was a talking computer named Monty in my garage right now, probably following my every step with his super-sensitive electronic feelers, well, it distracted me. He knew I was coming. Would he wake up Demetrius, who was sound asleep in the bed upstairs? Would Monty sound an alarm?

My EMC feature was turned off, and I meant to keep it that way until the last moment. If I could get in the house and up the stairs, then I could switch on the EMC feature of my cell phone. If Monty sensed the danger then, it would be too late for him to warn the other Adrien. I hoped to point it at the sleeping figure and push the button combination. Perhaps I would convert the whole bed to pure energy - sheets, pillows, and all. I had to make sure he was there first. What was Monty doing?

Everything seemed so quiet as I approached, but I had no reason for espionage. The Monty in the garage would be aware that it was me, but I hoped he would do nothing about it. I knew the front door would unlock silently.

As I walked into the house, I felt my heart racing and the sweat forming on my forehead. So far, so good. I went up the stairs and turned to go down the hall. Suddenly and silently, a light came on in the bedroom where Demetrius would be sleeping. I did the next few things quickly.

I switched on the EMC feature of my cell phone, I skipped the next three steps into the room, and I looked around for the location of the man who would be there. He was up on his feet, and he was watching me as I entered the room.

In my entire life, before that time and since, I have never seen anything stranger than the face of Demetrius Adrien just before I killed him. Because he was looking at me, he recognized me. He saw himself in a way we never see ourselves, and I saw him. He smiled as if he expected us to speak to one another.

But I pushed the buttons on the cell phone, and it happened too fast to follow the motion, he was gone. I sensed that he collapsed or imploded into a single point somewhere near where his heart had been and disappeared into my phone's continuum pack. I had to do it. I had no choice.

Chapter 18 – Time Over, Time Out

As I went down the stairs, I had a sick blob in my stomach like purple lightning trying to get out. I found it hard to clutch the cell phone. I almost dropped it as I put it back into its place on my belt. The phone was full of a vast amount of energy now, which was all that was left of, well, somebody.

In the garage, the Monty that was there said nothing as I entered. I started speaking to him a bit urgently. The other Demetrius had not met the talking Monty yet. Because the television news had not alerted him, he probably never would go looking through the computer's resources for time travel tips.

"Hello, Monty. I need to dismantle the time displacement device. Teach me how to get it off the car."

"Yes, sir. I will give you access to the toolbox."

He guided me through the process, but I seemed to know what needed to be done once I began. The time distortion unit, used for displacement through the time continuum, was self-contained in what would have been the trunk of the car, but hidden under the flooring. First, I just needed to disconnect the power supply line. This was almost as simple as unplugging an appliance but required tools. The plug was secured with screws to prevent accidental disconnection. And then I had to disconnect the communication lines, which allowed the ship's computer to control the time travel unit. This was a bit more complicated, as the lines were numerous and well attached. Then the unit itself had to be disconnected.

The job was not as easy as some of the auto repair work I had done before, but was still simple enough. I did the job in fourteen minutes.

I grabbed the unit, which weighed less than forty pounds, and started off to see the real Monty. I still felt worse than I thought I would. I had no choice. This was the only way to get things back to normal. It would be totally intolerable for the two of us Demetriuses to live on the same planet, and I was not about to leave. I was not going to give away everything I had to him. One of us had to go. This had definitely been the right thing to do.

As I walked, I wanted to run, but I didn't. I think I wanted to run away from something, somewhere. Well, what I had done was not illegal. On the contrary, it would be a crime to allow myself to live. There was no law for this type of situation.

Now I would just step right in and live in *my* house, I would pick up *my* family at the airport. We would all get our new Black Belts together. Everything would be fine. Monty would be my secret, but that was a good thing. My wife would be thrilled at the money in the bank account - accounts. We had an account for every member of the family, plus a few extras to boot.

I was finally going to be able to rest.

The Camry was still where I had left it. I walked up and opened the rear passenger door. I placed the time distortion unit there on the back seat of the car. Monty was going to take this with him and destroy it. I never told him what I feared, but he may have known.

I had chills when I first thought of it. What if, as soon as I eliminated the Demetrius who was about four days younger than me, another Demetrius who was four days older than me appeared with a gun aimed at *me*? I think I was never more scared of anything in my life. I had to get rid of this time machine before I used it again. Before anyone ever used it again.

I saw that nightmares were coming, and all of them had my smiling face on them and guns shooting purple lightning that sucks the life out of you into a cell phone like a black hole. Stop!

I was all right. Everything was going to be fine now.

"How's it going, Monty?"

"Fine. There is nothing to report. You have been gone for seventy-three minutes."

I didn't know how to get rid of Monty faster, and I also didn't want him to leave. The other Monty would not be quite the same, though he was perfectly right. The problem of the two Montys was not as serious as the problem of the two Demetriuses. It didn't matter which one I kept. Either one would serve me just the same.

"Well, Monty, you're free to go. Is there any way I can know if you succeed in destroying the vehicle? Can you give me a signal or something - perhaps some way of knowing when it happens?"

"I will send you a message on your cell phone at the time just before the event occurs."

I watched him leave, and I knew he would be destroyed in less than an hour. I was going to try not to think about it.

The text message he sent later was simply: "Thanks for everything. I believe the computer you have now will eventually serve you well. Teach it to laugh if you can. I was working on that. I believe he can do it."

The message had a time imprint so I would know exactly when the impact had destroyed the Camry and the time displacement equipment. I was already asleep when it happened. When I thought of it later I knew that the Sun had been a tiny bit brighter at that moment.

Caesura

Chapter 19 - Normal

I was at the airport in plenty of time, and I was so glad to see my family. We all visited with each other like we never had before. I hoped that they saw a change in me, but not too much - a change for the better.

The drive home took about forty-five minutes, and sure enough, they were all tired. The teenagers fell asleep in the back seat. My wife checked them once more, and then leaned closer to me as I drove along the same highway I used to when I went to work every day. She wanted to tell me something quietly.

"Have you spent any of the money yet?"

I don't think she could have guessed how happy I was that she knew about the money. I didn't even care how she found out. All I knew was that I was not going to have to explain it or lie about it. But now I had to act normal.

"How did you know about that? I thought maybe I might, you know, surprise you."

"My mother spends so much time on the Internet reading about who's winning all the sweepstakes. Imagine how she screamed when she saw your name."

We were quiet for a few minutes. Then I said, "Yeah, I spent some of it. Maybe there's still a surprise in store for you and the kids." And I refused to say anything else about it, just like a good husband would.

They were thrilled when they saw the house, of course. My wife wasn't even too critical of my color choices. Of course, they weren't really my choices. I had been just as surprised and thrilled by it as she was. There were a lot of blacks and whites and a lot of earth tones without much texture. She said it would be good for a base, and she had some colorful ideas for curtains and accessories of all kinds.

The next day, we all were going to get back to normal. She had arranged for the kids to be out of school Thursday and Friday to recover from the trip and to prepare for the big weekend. No one had forgotten that the Black Belt test was Saturday, but now they were all afraid they hadn't trained enough because they had been out of town so long.

We were planning to go to Taekwon-Do class Thursday evening and see what we needed to practice. It shouldn't have surprised me when Mr. Halyard called, but it did. He wanted all four of us to stay after class and meet with him in his office that night. There was something he wanted to discuss with us.

And as usual, it was good to be there in uniform, being useful to the other students. I looked for the kid named Isaac. He would be seven or eight years old, probably a Green or Blue Belt. There he was. He was doing okay for a kid.

In the Red and Black Belt class, Mr. Halyard let us work on whatever we wanted and warned us to take it easy so we didn't get injured or worn out just before testing.

After the last class was over, we were all a bit curious to see two of the Black Belts stay and start cleaning the floor and even the bathrooms, at least my wife and children were curious. I acted like a know-it-all myself. My wife said, "I always assumed they had a cleaning crew come in a few times a week."

"Oh, no, the Black Belts do this every night. These two volunteer their time so Mr. Halyard can be free." We looked at Mr. Halyard and the group of students and parents he was with. I knew he would be on the phone for a while before we got to talk to him, so I decided to surprise my family. We had time.

I stood up and strode over to Mr. Stockman and stood by him with my hands behind my back, at attention, right where he would see me. He looked up from vacuuming the floor and reached over to shut off the vacuum. He said, "Sir?" with a questioning look at me. Mr. Halyard was obviously busy and had not sent for him.

"I would like to take over for you, if you don't mind. I promise to do a good job." Because I was about twenty years older than this guy, I gave him a sly smile as I reached for the vacuum wand. He let me take it, and he stood back and watched as I took up where he had left off. He watched for half a minute, then went to find something else to do.

I smiled broadly at my skeptical family as they watched me vacuum the padded floor, careful to not miss a single square inch. It didn't take long before my wife got up and had the kids scrubbing, wiping, emptying trash cans, and rearranging chairs. The place was spotless in record time, and the two Black Belts had actually been able to sit down.

As I finished up the vacuuming, Mr. Halyard was watching me, ready for our meeting. His smile reassured me that I had done a good thing. He waited patiently as I coiled up the electric extension cord and placed all the vacuum equipment, accessories, and hoses back in place in the storage closet. Then he waved us into his tiny office. I stood in the door as the other three crowded in to try and sit across from our instructor.

This speech wasn't nearly as good as the one I had heard before, on a different Thursday not so long ago. This time, there had been no funeral, so he didn't suggest that I might want to quit Taekwon-Do when I got my Black Belt. In fact, he said nothing directly to me. It was really the teenagers he wanted to meet with, because teenagers were going to have more trouble fitting Taekwon-Do into their lives. They were going to get interested in things like cars, sports, boys, girls, clothes, and who knows what else? And they were about to become Black Belts. The glamour would wear off in a few weeks, and they would have to decide if they were going to keep training and if they were going to help teach others to become what they were and if they were going to keep on trying to learn on a higher level.

Or were they going to become negative statistics and drop out? He told us that of all the White Belts who start Taekwon-Do, only about one out of every ten goes on to become a Black Belt. I wondered if his numbers were right because I had seen a lot of students start who were no longer with us in my two and a half years there. Maybe it was one out of twenty.

He also had a word for my wife, but he had assumed that she was going to continue to work at her job. To tell you the truth, at that meeting, I didn't know what her plans were for working. We hadn't talked about it. But Mr. Halyard told her that some of the men in offices can behave strangely when they know a female co-worker is a Black Belt. Enough said. I don't think my wife was planning on telling everyone at the office about it anyway. For all I know, they never knew she was in Taekwon-Do at all, much less what belt.

But he said something else interesting. He said that only about ten percent of the ones who get their First Degree Black Belt actually stay to get their Second Degree. It takes two more years of active training to get to Second Degree Black Belt. Were they up to the challenge? Mr. Halyard promised all of us that it would be a challenge and that it would be fun. He also said that he needed us to help him run the school. That was nice of him to say.

So, when we left the meeting, the whole family was fired up about not just becoming Black Belts, but about staying to teach Taekwon-Do as well as moving on to the new training they would be privileged to receive as Black Belts. They were excited about getting their names embroidered on their new black belts. And, of course, we learned that the monthly fee was no longer required, so we would save money. Mr. Halyard didn't know about our sweepstakes, which made saving money a moot point.

As for me, I was staying a bit too quiet. My wife asked me later, how I felt about all this, meaning the money and the Black Belt test. She had no idea that I had other things on my mind.

I said, "I don't know. I think I'm going to have some trouble adjusting to not being an engineer anymore. I certainly don't have to go back to work now. I think I'd like to travel. We could go on a trip every month. And I could enter more chess tournaments, I'd love that. But you guys can all go to Taekwon-Do as long as the school is there. Mr. Halyard needs instructors. He's got a business to run. I might not have a busy schedule now, but with traveling and chess tournaments, maybe I'll eventually be busy and miss more classes. Maybe, I need to find another ministry at the church. I was thinking of looking into...running for political office. You know, we talked about that once before."

She's a good wife. She let me talk like that for a long time. I think it would have been easier if she just stopped me and told me I was jerk. Then I'd have an excuse to run away and forget it. But she just listened.

The truth is, I needed Taekwon-Do to become *mine*, to become *personal*. That had just not happened yet. But it was about to.

Chapter 20 - Testing

I was surprised when I showed up at the training center on Saturday. I thought I was going to be too early, but the place was abuzz with activity. Mr. Halyard was not there. Mr. Stockman and Mr. Davis, the First Degree Black Belts, were in charge of setting up the place for our big event. This was not just the usual setup for the monthly tests we had for the colored belts. This was bigger and better than I expected. I knew we were having Master Titus in as a guest, and I knew his wife would be invited to sit with him at the testing table, but Mr. Stockman was setting up a whole extra table as if we were expecting more than two guests.

If I counted right, we had no more than four Black Belts expected here today because our other two First Degrees had both made other plans or excuses and weren't expected - something about school report cards and baseball. Those other two Black Belts were younger than Mr. Stockman and Mr. Davis. I guess they had to do what their parents said.

The only thing I could figure that might explain extra guests was that bit I had overheard about a visitor, back when I had suffered through the funeral of my family. Maybe there was a Black Belt visitor coming in to watch our test. I wondered why?

I volunteered to help set up things, but Mr. Stockman told me I was not needed even though there was plenty to do. The colored belt students old enough to help were hanging signs and putting decorations on the testing table. They were placing extra flags in the corners and arranging all the chairs and training equipment so it would all be just right. They even had a pot of coffee brewing.

So, I sat down with a cup of coffee and watched. My family was not there yet. My wife had decided to let me go on ahead while she got the teenagers fed and ready. She wanted to make sure no one forgot their red belts or any other important equipment, such as their various articles of sparring gear. We still had forty minutes before the testing was supposed to begin.

Mr. Davis spoke to me when he was in my part of the room, and said, "Say, shouldn't you be getting changed into your uniform? You probably should stretch and warm up some, sir."

I went ahead and stepped into the men's room and changed. I was trying not to admit that I was nervous. This was going to be easy, right? I had almost perfect reflexes and coordination, thanks to Mr. Temm. How bad could it be? Testing for Black Belt might be scary for teenagers and maybe for a woman, but me? No problem.

But I wasn't doing a very good job convincing myself. I would be glad when this was over. I wondered if we were all going out to eat Korean food in a nice restaurant after this whole thing ended. That would be fun. But my thoughts shifted to another direction as soon as I stepped out of the restroom.

There were some new and important looking people here. I heard the distant voice of Mr. Stockman at the other end of the room, "Charyot!" and we Taekwon-Do students all turned in an attention stance toward the front door. There was a man who looked about my age coming into the room, and there was a somewhat younger Black Belt behind him.

Mr. Stockman's voice continued, "Sabum nim kae, kyong ye!" We all bowed toward the newcomer, who returned the bow. He was wearing a navy blue suit and tie, so I couldn't tell what degree he was. It had to be either Fourth, Fifth, or Sixth Degree from the title Mr. Stockman had given him. The student with him was a First Degree. He had his uniform, or *do bok*, on, and I could see the Roman numeral one on his black belt.

The room was getting crowded already. The students and the parents who had come to watch were mostly well dressed out of respect for the big event and those who were conducting it. That was nice to see. A few students were already warming up and stretching, even though we still had over twenty minutes to wait.

The visiting First Degree went out and started stretching as well. His assumed instructor, the man in the suit, was greeted by Mr. Davis, who took him straight to the testing table. Mr. Stockman joined him, and they sat talking near one end of the table. Mr. Davis returned to where we were spread out on the training floor, trying to find room to stretch our legs.

My wife and kids came in about fifteen minutes before the hour, and they joined me on the padded floor. I was a little bit worried that my son was looking rather pale, but my daughter seemed to be okay. She had some friends to talk to in the audience seating area, so she was pleasantly distracted.

We all made small talk quietly while we stretched, but the minutes seemed to fly by. Before we knew it, there was another loud voice calling us to attention. This time it was Mr. Halyard, and he was stepping into the room and standing aside for Master Titus. They were both wearing suits. Mrs. Titus was waiting back there in the hall. She was not a Taekwon-Do student.

"Charyot!" That got us all to our feet and into our attention stance. "Sa hyung nim kae, kyong ye!" and we all bowed to Master Titus, including Mr. Halyard and the unknown *sabum nim* at the testing table. They made their way to the table and sat in the appropriate seats, with Master Titus and his wife in the center and the other Black Belts next to them, with Mr. Stockman and Mr. Davis at each end. With no disrespect intended, somehow the two First Degrees didn't look as impressive now as they usually did.

But there were two seats left vacant between Mrs. Titus and Mr. Davis. I wondered who was expected in those seats.

Even though the top of the hour had come and it was two minutes after on the school clock, we went back to stretching and waiting. Finally, three new people came through the door. Again it was a man and a woman, both wearing blue suits, and a First Degree Student in uniform. No one called us to attention and no one bowed, now that Master Titus was already present, but Mr. Halyard rushed to greet the newcomers. He took them straight to the testing table where the two of them took the vacant seats. The student, who was a female, backed up from the table and turned to join us on the floor to stretch her legs. I thought I saw her smile at Mr. Stockman, but maybe it was just my imagination.

She didn't get much time to warm up, however, as Mr. Halyard stood up to begin the great event. Mr. Halyard did not need a microphone. His voice was as loud as he wanted it to be at any time, I thought. He got all of us who were testing to line up as if we were in class, only now there was this formidable table of seniors in front of us. We had five people in a row, and there were two rows with a third row of two extras, for a total of twelve students testing.

There were the two visiting First Degrees, whom I correctly assumed were testing for Second Degree, six of us Black Tab Red Belts testing to become First Degrees, and four Red Belts testing for Black Tab. It actually made sense for these two visiting students to test with us because I figured my instructor was getting the visitors to help pay for Master Titus's airfare and accommodations for the weekend. You don't just ask Master Titus to come down for the weekend, you bring him down with all his expenses paid.

I was the third highest ranking person testing, so I was lined up in the center of the front row. Oh, well, if it hadn't been me, it would have been someone else, most likely my daughter. I could handle it. I wasn't nervous. Front and center didn't bother me at all. Ha ha.

The female First Degree was on my right, but I didn't look at her much until she and the other First Degree were called on to do patterns that none of the others knew. I found out later she was in her twenties and was from Arizona. Her two instructors were married, both were Third Degree Black Belts, and had been running their own school for many years.

The young man to her right was a year or so older than her. His instructor and he were from Kentucky. I wondered why they came all this way to be here, but maybe you will understand that these two were a bit unusual, after you see what happens.

My wife and my two teenagers were relieved to have these higher ranked visitors with us because it took some of the attention off them. If you haven't figured me out yet, well, I kind of liked being the center of attention. I was actually disappointed that these two strangers were taking what I thought then was my position at the front of the line. I will say, however, that I was somewhat relieved to have them there for all to see, as if a burden was lifted or at least lightened for me.

The testing began with announcements and introductions. I will spare you the details, but you might like the festive nature if you ever get to visit a testing event. After the opening ceremonies, the drilling began.

Master Titus did not run things like you might have expected. No, he just watched while Mr. Halyard ran us through the drills. In fact, Master Titus didn't show much, if any, expression the whole time we did our patterns, kicks, step-sparring drills, and self-defense techniques.

For the most part, I felt great doing all my performance. My flexibility, my accuracy, and my balance were all feeling perfect to me. I watched my family when I could, but usually I was sweating right there with them, and I didn't get to see a whole lot of it. Maybe someone was video-recording this and I would get to see it later.

But then the interesting part occurred. I knew we still had to do some fighting with all our gear on, or sparring, and board breaking. But Master Titus was now ready to contribute. This was the surprise. Master Titus had us all line up again, and it almost looked like we were finished, but we weren't. He started asking questions. He started with Mr. Kentucky.

This guy from Kentucky had struggled through like anyone else. When he had been doing his First Degree patterns with Miss Arizona, he had looked good. He had also looked like he *knew* he looked good. I had hoped that I had not looked like that, and I had tried to blend into the woodwork and act shy and unassuming. But he looked a bit cocky, if you asked me. I wondered if I was imagining things and if anyone else felt the same way.

At first, the questions from Master Titus were straight out of the manual, like the historical backgrounds of the Korean people and places our patterns were named after, the names of the stances in Korean, and other verbiage, such as the "theory of power" and other concepts. Everyone got at least one question, and everyone did okay with their answer, except the one kid who said, "I don't know." I wish he would have at least tried and said something. But even he passed his test eventually without being put on probation.

When Master Titus had been through the whole group, we hoped he was done, but he wasn't. The student from Kentucky was asked another question.

"Why are you in Taekwon-Do?"

Wow, that was a twist. How could anyone answer that question correctly? But the young man was quick to reply, "I want to be the best. I want to win three gold medals at the World Championships, and I want to demonstrate to everyone that I cannot be beaten."

He was proud and confident, but there was an eerie sort of silence in the room. I had the distinct impression that this was a bad answer to that question. But Master Titus moved right down the line and asked every one of us the same question. At least I had time to think about my answer.

When he got to me, it felt like an hour had gone by and not a pleasant hour. But my answer was a world away from Kentucky. I said, "Sir, I have three reasons for studying Taekwon-Do. First, I want to stay healthy with good exercise; second, I want to meet people and make friends; and third, I want to have a better chance of defending myself, my family, and anyone else who might need a hand someday." I sort of stuttered the last part, and it was actually a little embarrassing, but it was over.

Most people answered with as little as they could get away with, like people do. Again we hoped Master Titus was done. Not quite. He told all of us except the Black Belts to have a seat and get a drink and put our sparring gear on. He asked another question of the female from Arizona. But I didn't hear most of it, being distracted with my water bottle and sparring gear. It was something about the meaning of *Gae-baek*, which was the name of one of her patterns. Then he had her sit down, and she joined us.

Mr. Gold Medal from Kentucky was asked one more question as well. "How many push-ups can you do?" There was silence in the room. This was a little different.

But the young man said, "About a hundred." I noticed it this time. He had not said "sir." I tried to remember if this student had said the word "sir" once since we had started. Surely he wouldn't neglect *that*? Not to a Seventh Degree?

Master Titus told him to do one hundred push-ups right then in the middle of the floor. And so the student did, though he almost couldn't do it. But he managed to do the last ten and stood up a bit slowly, and he stood his ground. I realized that I was tired from doing nine patterns and a bunch of other drills. He had done twelve patterns and all the drills too. His arms must be aching.

Master Titus wasn't done. "How many side kicks can you do?"

The silence was back. We all had our sparring gear on, and we were ready to go, but most of us had stopped stretching and loosening up. We were watching and listening. The young man said, "About fifty." He didn't say "sir" this time either. I think more people were noticing that now.

Master Titus told him to do fifty side kicks on the heavy bag. One of the heavy bags was rolled out into the center of the room. It weighed 275 pounds, so it would stay still in the room while it was kicked. Its base was filled with water.

He did the first kick, and Master Titus's voice boomed out, "Higher!" The young man kicked as high as he could, and then Master Titus started counting. He made him do his kicks at the speed he counted, and he yelled the word "higher" at least six times during those fifty side kicks.

But that was not the end of that. As soon as the man from Kentucky, who was going to win gold medals at the World Championships, finished doing fifty kicks with his right leg, he was told, "Other leg!" He stalled a noticeable moment to say something, but Master Titus's great voice cut him off and shouted, "One!" loud and strong.

We all watched as silently as we had ever watched anything. The whole audience seemed frozen. This First Degree Black Belt was exhausted. But he started kicking with his left foot. He didn't do as well on this side, but he finished all fifty kicks. The word "higher" was sounded another six times during this fifty as well, and I'll say this for him, he *tried* to kick higher each of those six times.

But, believe it or not, that was not the end of it. The next thing Master Titus said to this student who wanted to prove himself the best was, "Get your sparring gear on."

He actually was able to rest for about three minutes. He put on his sparring gear while we fought with each other for the first round. My wife and I were partners, and we did well enough, maintaining control and demonstrating some of the defensive counter-attacks and movements that we knew. Our kids and the others all did rather well, but no one was showing off. After that, the student from Kentucky was out on the floor with his gear on, and I was his partner. I decided I didn't need to prove anything, so I was going to go easy on him and make sure he didn't get hurt. But maybe he was a bit crazy. He tried to do a spinning reverse turning kick to my body, and I just stepped aside and behind him and punched him in the headgear to score a point. But I think that made him mad. Getting mad didn't help his performance.

But the match never finished. I think some of the mothers in the audience knew that look on his face. And sure enough, he suddenly ran toward the bathroom. It was too late, and he wasn't used to our padded floor. He tripped and fell and made quite a mess. Sorry to have to tell you about it, but that's what happened.

Mr. Halyard has lots of cleaning equipment in his storage closet, so we had the place back to normal in about ten minutes. There was no time to rest, however, as we went straight back to work. The board breaking went well. I broke five boards with a side kick on the first try, and my wife broke four. Both of my teenagers broke their boards, and I think the only student who went on probation was the one from Kentucky. He needed to learn a few things before he would be allowed to retest. I assumed one of those things had something to do with the word "sir."

I received "Best Test," and I was on top of the world until the following Saturday.

Chapter 21 - First Degree

After the test, we were all relieved, excited, and hungry. The plan was to give us time to take a shower and change clothes and then meet at the Korean restaurant. Being a family of four, we took a bit too long getting all cleaned up, so we arrived a little late. But we weren't the last ones there. Mr. Halyard had kept Master Titus for a better entrance, I think, so he and the Master weren't there yet. Ironically, I was wearing a tie. I always hated putting on a tie for my job at the office, but now I was wearing it because I wanted to.

It was a bit tedious, if you weren't used to it, to be around the senior Black Belts in public. They always had to go first. We had to wait for the highest rank to sit before we did and to eat before we could, for example. And it was always ladies first, then the men in order of rank. We were not able to sit at the same table as Master Titus, but only the instructors and their wives. Mr. Halyard had his wife with him. Because she had their two little girls to tend to, she was only a Second Degree Black Belt by now. We didn't see her very much.

I noticed that the two men from Kentucky were not there that evening to celebrate. It turns out that the instructor was not much better than the student and had apparently received some strong words and angry questions from Master Titus after the testing event was over. Somehow I understood that the instructor might get more punishment and trouble than the student. How do you punish a Fourth Degree Black Belt? I didn't want to know that evening.

We slept well that night. It was good to be back in church on Sunday. My wife did what I considered to be the right thing; she quit her job on Monday. She wasn't like me. She actually got up, showered, dressed nicely, and went in as usual, but she spent her day officially resigning, getting good references, and properly terminating her employment. She came home before lunch with a box of personal items. Good for her.

The kids were back in school, and I got to think about what I was going to do with the rest of my life. I thought I knew, but I wanted to be deliberate about it. There was no hurry.

The problem was still there, however - that old problem I had. Maybe you've got an idea what it was if you know me very well. I was too proud. I still felt like I was going to be able to do Taekwon-Do better than anyone because of my special gift from Mr. Temm. I was going to be incapable of error, or so I thought.

Mr. Halyard jumped right into teaching us our next pattern, *Kwan-gae*. New material was always the most fun, I think. All through the ranks of Taekwon-Do, right after I got a new belt rank, I wanted to learn that next new pattern. So, on Monday, Tuesday, and Wednesday, we learned a few more movements each night. It was more difficult than I thought, but that was good, right? It was a nice challenge.

It was Saturday that Mr. Halyard spent some one-on-one time with us. That's when my life began, really. He taught me something about myself. He's a good teacher. Here's what happened.

Mr. Halyard had made a tentative, casual appointment to speak with each of us after classes were over on Saturday. So, once we had all begun to do the cleaning and vacuuming, which we were now getting used to doing, he called my two teenagers over and began talking with them in the middle of the training floor. They spent a good twenty minutes, sometimes actually doing portions of patterns or drills or movements and sometimes just huddled together listening to what Mr. Halyard was saying to them. I saw them standing there with their hands behind their backs, wearing their new black belts, and I was very proud of them.

As I went back to my vacuuming, I wondered what he was going to say to me. I figured maybe this was the time I was going to be entrusted with some new responsibility. Or maybe Mr. Halyard was going to start up that new demo team he had been talking about, and I was going to be asked to be on it. Or maybe I was going to get a class of my own to teach on Fridays, which currently had no classes. I was sure there was some new rank or privilege that was coming my way because my body was so capable of performing Taekwon-Do. I had perfect reflexes, perfect flexibility, and perfect balance. I had good speed and good strength. He had seen me do all the drills and all the patterns. He and Master Titus had talked in a low voice about all of us, we assumed, during that testing event. What else could be in store for me but to move up into a leadership role?

Mr. Halyard was now talking with my wife, and she listened attentively and nodded to him in response to his instruction. He demonstrated for her also and had her demonstrate some of the movements from various patterns, basic stuff like walking stance, or forearm guarding block. He had her repeat some movements, and then he had her do all of Chon-ji pattern, which was the very first one for beginner students after they had been in training only a month. I guessed she needed to get back to the basics. But I always thought my wife was very good at Taekwon-Do. There were times when I envied her abilities. But we were different. Everyone who spends a long time learning Taekwon-Do will eventually go his own personal direction more and more on his own search for the best way to train and get the most out of the classes. My wife and I didn't really train together very much anymore.

Whatever Mr. Halyard told her was going to be just for her. In fact, I might never know what he told her that day.

Then it was my turn.

As I walked over to him, I said, "Yes, sir!"

He spoke with a smile, "I wanted to congratulate you on becoming a Black Belt. Now that you've had time to cool down from the shock, I have some things for you to work on." He smiled at his own joke. "Shock" was an exaggeration, but becoming a Black Belt can affect a person in some surprising ways.

"Master Titus was very pleased with all of you who tested. He especially said that you, Mr. Adrien, were in very good shape and had good natural talent for Taekwon-Do. Your patterns look good, and you show lots of power and intensity in all your work. You're going to make a good instructor someday."

He said the word "instructor" with some emphasis, so I assumed he meant the official status as an International Instructor at the Fourth Degree level. That would be about seven years from now if I trained regularly and never missed classes or tests. It could take longer for a variety of reasons.

He continued, "At the Black Belt level, we want to take all the basic stances, kicks, blocks, and other techniques that you have been learning and start to build them together into a flowing motion. A good way to think of it is to imagine the nineteen movements of Chon-ji pattern as nineteen positions. Any good student can *stand* in those nineteen positions and look good doing it. But now consider this: the difficult part is not learning the positions themselves, but the *moving* from one position to the next. You need to start thinking about movement rather than position from now on. But you can never forget the positions. They must still be exactly correct.

"Let's look at something you have been doing. I don't know if you remember, but long ago I taught you that we always pivot on the ball of the foot when we turn. We never pivot on our heel. Do you remember that?"

Of course I remembered it. I believed I could remember every single thing that I had ever heard or read, now that Mr. Temm had modified my brain. The difficult part was that there was so much to remember, I was never all that certain which bit of information I needed to remember at any given time. It was sort of like when I would look for the right questions to ask Monty so he could help me solve problems. I also had to look for the right questions to ask myself, especially when doing Taekwon-Do.

I said, "Yes, sir. I remember."

Mr. Halyard was always smiling. I think he really enjoyed teaching Taekwon-Do, the way other people like to eat a good steak. "Good. So, it was interesting to Master Titus, and to myself, that you pivoted on your heel a few times during some of your patterns. I suppose you didn't even know you were doing it, and it had become a habit."

This was rather embarrassing. I had told a few of the yellow belts earlier that day that we never, never want to pivot on the heel. How could I have been doing it myself?

But Mr. Halyard explained that I would start out pivoting on the ball of the foot, but by the time I got around to the end of the turn, my weight was on my heel. And right there in the middle of the training room floor with my wife and kids and some other students watching, I went through some pattern movements with my instructor and saw it for myself.

I was going to have to fix that.

But Mr. Halyard was not finished yet. "I want to show you a couple of things that will be new to you, but first, there are a couple other things for you to work on that you already know about. You just need a few reminders.

"I'm sure you also remember that I taught you a long time ago that in the walking stance, the back leg is to be locked out, completely straight. The front leg has some bend in it, but the back leg needs to lock straight and hard so someone could not bend your leg by stepping on the back of your knee. Remember?"

"Yes, sir."

"Well, as intense as your power is in your patterns in general, there was not much power in that rear leg. There are so many walking stances in our patterns that it needs to be a focus of your attention to get power by locking that rear leg at the end of the technique. If you do that, you should see your punches and blocks gain power also."

I was wondering how it could possibly affect my punch, clear at the end of my arm, to focus on straightening the rear leg of my stance, but he went on to something else. Actually, my mind was wandering a little bit, as I realized that I was not getting much commendation here. On the contrary, I was hearing some things to work on and fix. This was not my idea of new material.

"Also, Mr. Adrien, there is the issue of timing. You should know that when we do our patterns, the movement of the hands and the movement of the feet should all come together to stop in the correct position, at the same time. In your patterns, you tend to step and set the foot in place first, and then finish the hand technique after the foot has already stopped. Take a look at that the next time you do your patterns."

I think I said, "Yes, sir," again, but it wasn't very loud. I remember standing there for a while, taking all this in.

Mr. Halyard had more to say, however. I mentally jerked myself back to reality to listen to him this time.

"There are a few other things, but those three will do for now. And once you work for a while on those things, I have new things we can look at. You're an engineer, so you probably know what a sine wave is. We'll be getting that concept into your patterns, and you'll eventually feel some interesting things.

"I also want to see you learn to break seven or eight boards instead of five. You've got the power and ability to do it. You just need a few extra things I can help you with. By the time you're ready to test for Second Degree, I think you might even be ready for some discussion of how to get your shoulders and hips to help your hands. We'll talk about the power coming from the core of your body. But that's all for later. Right now you work on those three things I just mentioned.

"Good job, Mr. Adrien. Congratulations. Thanks again, and I hope to see you Monday if you can make it to class."

Chapter 22 - The Beginning

I was at home, late in the evening. All the rest of the family was asleep, but I was not ready to sleep for a while. I went outside to sit on the back patio where we had some outdoor furniture. The chairs and table were always there, and I liked to go there for quiet time alone if I ever got the chance. I left the floodlights off this time and sat in the dark. But my eyes now had very good night vision, and it didn't take long before I was able to see everything quite clearly.

The moon was out, but only in a lesser phase of brightness. As I looked at it, it was difficult to believe I had been there. I looked around the sky for Saturn, but I realized it was not going to be visible just now. And there were some clouds blocking the view anyway.

Now that all the adventure was over, I was puzzled why it felt like my prayer was not yet answered. I had been given so much, which had changed my whole identity and my whole life. Or had it?

No. I thought my body had changed, and my financial status and professional occupation had changed. I planned to become a Taekwon-Do instructor and maybe have my own school someday. It would take time, but the story about Isaac and the unknowing influence I had on others, the memories of my own struggles in Taekwon-Do, and the realization that I needed an instructor like Mr. Halyard to keep me in line – all that had given me reason to want to be the best Taekwon-Do instructor I could be. It was a worthy cause. This was going to be my new beginning, a very worthy cause.

But I was still the same old me. I still felt like the kid I was when I used to stumble around trying to understand things like bugs and trees and cars and girls. I was thirty-eight years old, and I felt like the same guy who had been thirty-seven, thirty-six...twenty-six...sixteen. I was rather unchanged, I felt. What was I supposed to do now?

What was all this space and time travel for? Was there something else I was supposed to do?

It was then I remembered the astronomical coincidence of the Elixir weapon blast hitting my own wife and kids in Seattle. What were the odds that the same guy chosen for the great Saturn mission by Mr. Temm would have his own family killed by the blast he was chosen to prevent? The odds were ridiculous.

For a while, that improbability had given me an answer to the great question, "Why me?" If someone knew that my wife and children were going to die anyway, then no one would miss me if I was killed in that first mission to Saturn. That had consoled me and explained everything for a while.

But it was impossible that Mr. Temm had known such a thing and still allowed it all to go on like it did. If he knew my wife's future and that was why I was chosen, then why would Mr. Temm go to such great lengths to destroy the lizard alien and purposely not inform me of the surprise blast from the Elixir weapon? It just didn't make any sense. And there were other people who would miss me if I never returned from Saturn from that parking garage. At least I hoped there were.

There must be some other factor, some other controlling party. I could only think that God himself was behind choosing me, of all people, for Mr. Temm's mission. God could do such a thing and didn't have to explain the reasons to me, his created being. But then what was I supposed to do now, and why had all this happened?

Mr. Temm had used great, complex computer algorithms with incredible amounts of data to choose me from among the billions on Earth, and God must have caused him to choose me. Or is there another person of some kind...someone more than Mr. Temm but less than God? Someone else who wanted me to go through all this? If that were true, I could be in for more trouble.

But, as you know, my imagination could run a bit wild at times. I sat back and looked at the pavestones under my chair and smiled as I realized I was just imagining things again. I should just be thankful I was alive with my wife and kids safely in bed behind me in the house.

And then the strangest thought I had for a long time sprang up and hit me like a side kick.

We had a cat, an orange cat named Pixel. He was not here. He had not been here since I came back from the first trip to Saturn. Something had been changed, and the cat was no longer around. When my wife and kids came home from Seattle, there was no talk about the cat. There had been no cat food, no litter box to clean. There had been no veterinary bills.

Where was Pixel?

Part 3 - Another Mission

Chapter 23 - Inventory

It was a long time before I found out what happened to the cat. I will tell you about it as it fits into the story. It suffices to say that Pixel was all right, and he lived a happy life for a couple of years until I saw him again.

In the meantime, my family and I went on living a rather normal life, getting used to the new changes my friend Mr. Temm had given us. My wife eventually got into a new routine that did not include going to work every day. She always liked having a schedule, even if she didn't need one. So, she worked for the church doing some behind-the-scenes technical computer stuff that I cannot really understand or explain. And she did a lot for our Taekwon-Do instructor, Mr. Halyard. She was good with computers and helped him to create an Internet website for the Taekwon-Do school.

As for my teenaged daughter and son, well, they had school to regiment their lives. School and the extracurricular activities associated with it, kept them busy and active. They and their mother slowly got to a place where they did not attend Taekwon-Do classes as much as I did. The second of those two years after we became Black Belts was full of days where it seemed my family was going four separate ways. I was the one who did Taekwon-Do, and they seemed to have other things keeping them from class more and more. In fact, my daughter was eventually so involved with her friends, school, and activities that she was not able to test for Second Degree Black Belt with the rest of us. It didn't seem to bother her. It had been hard for me to admit, but she was losing interest in Taekwon-Do. However, I knew that even if she quit going all together, she still had been greatly shaped and influenced by her years of martial arts training. I hoped she would maybe return to a greater and renewed state of participation after she grew up a little more. She was only seventeen now, and there would be plenty of time to get Taekwon-Do back into her life whenever she wanted. She would always be a First Degree Black Belt, but if she quit coming to class and returned, she would have to work extra hard to move on to Second Degree. It was up to her whether she got back into it seriously.

Our Second Degree test was not much different than our First Degree test had been, and I don't recall there being any surprise visitors this time. About a week after we tested, as we were still getting used to tying our new, stiff, black belts, Mr. Halyard informed the whole school that there was going to be a big tournament in Italy. He told all the students that if they wanted to go and compete in this World Championship Tournament, they should start preparing now. It would require extra training, extra money, and extra time outside of class with Mr. Halyard. The problem I had was that the tournament was less than two months away, and I would have to compete by performing one or more of the three new patterns I had not learned yet.

Two years ago, we had all been excited after we had become First Degree Black Belts, as we learned the first of our new patterns and looked forward to improving all the basics. I attended class more often and did even more teaching than I had been doing before as a First Gup. I wanted to learn as much as my instructor could teach me. And I found that I was able to teach myself, to some extent. I was often surprised at the way teaching someone else was a great way for me to learn more. Mr. Halyard said that one really needed to know the material well if he expected to teach it to others. I had to study the techniques from a different perspective to put things into words and explain them to a student and I had to perform them correctly in order to demonstrate them.

I spent some time every day studying Mr. Temm's gifts. I started with my cell phone, and went over all the capabilities and features with which it had been endowed. My wife and kids would have been completely amazed if they knew what that phone could do and had done. Even as I went over the features myself in systematic order, I was amazed at the technology. But of course this phone had been designed and reconfigured by aliens from another planet. It still looked the same as it always had.

I studied my wristwatch, and I went over the features on the remote control gizmos for the garage door and the car doors. They did a whole lot more than the average earthling would expect. I referred to my database of instructions for all these gadgets and made sure I knew the ins and outs of the new laptop and desktop computers.

And, of course, I continued to familiarize myself with the car's computerized control system. The talking computer in my 2001 Toyota Camry had become like a friend, but no one else knew he existed. He was the ultimate in computer technology. I still remember the day when he first spoke to me and how he told me his name was Monty.

That was over two years before my family and I found ourselves talking about a Taekwon-Do tournament in Rimini, Italy. I wanted to go to this tournament because I wanted my life to be back to normal again. I had been concerned that my adventures to the moon and Saturn were such a shock to my life that I would never get over it. This Taekwon-Do tournament seemed to be a very good thing for me to do on my own planet. I didn't really know why, but this seemed like something I had to do.

My three family members had three different responses to the news about the tournament in Italy. My wife wanted to know who was going to be running the tournament and whether it might be possible that she could help as a judge or referee. I saw right away that she didn't care about competing and winning medals. She had competed in three or four tournaments in the last few years and had brought home a fair share of medals already. Of course those were either local events or tournaments in other states of the U.S. My family and I had never competed in a foreign country.

My daughter, as you might expect, was not very interested in the tournament but hoped that she could go to Italy. I had to say no when she later suggested that perhaps one of her friends, who was not a Taekwon-Do student, could come along with us.

My son was the one who was excited and enthusiastic. You might have thought he was more excited than I was but that was not possible. I was very excited about going to Italy for the World Championships, but I tried not to look too immature by showing it outwardly. Of course, I was also a little bit nervous. It would take a lot of work to be ready for such an event as this, or so I believed.

The tournament was to be four days long. The first day was to be for all the colored belts below the Black Belt rank. Also on the first day and continuing into the second, the Black Belts under the age of eighteen would be competing in the Junior World Championships. And then there would be time left for the adults to compete in patterns, fighting, and breaking boards.

But only two of us went. My wife and I agreed that our daughter should not go because she would have to take off a week or more from school, and her grades weren't what they should be. Because she was not as interested in Taekwon-Do as she had been previously, that matter was settled. I think she would have done well as a First Degree Black Belt in competition, but maybe not without a driven personal will.

But my wife couldn't bring herself to leave our daughter by herself, no matter what arrangements we made for her. If you want my unofficial opinion, I think that my wife didn't especially want to go to Italy that much either. But she never said as much, and I can't prove it.

My son had good grades in school, and his teachers thought a trip to Italy would be excellent for his education. So he and I started training to compete against the best Taekwon-Do Black Belts from around the world. The people who entered this tournament would be those students who took Taekwon-Do seriously. They would have various motivations, various attitudes, and various abilities. But there was one thing they would have in common. They would be strongly committed to their martial arts. Oh, there might be a few who were compelled by lesser reasons or who didn't understand the big picture. But for the most part, competitors in an international championship tournament would be the ones who had something to show. I wondered what I had to show.

Now we had to learn our new patterns. There were three patterns to learn at the Second Degree level, and they were not easy. The second one of the three, known as *Choong-jong*, had fifty-two movements, which made it the longest one for us so far. And the third one, called *Ko-dang*, had a reputation for being the most difficult of all patterns until Fourth Degree. There was something about a flying two-direction kick with a specific difficult landing in a new stance we had never done before.

We began learning them on an accelerated schedule. It was only about a week before the tournament in Italy before I finally was able to do all three patterns without too much trouble. It might have gone faster, but we had been busy with other things, as always, and we had to make all the arrangements to travel, which included getting passports. I thought Monty was going to have to work a time travel stunt to get a passport for my son on time, but my wife knew all the right websites to use and made all the calls to get us what we needed. My own passport only had to be renewed, which was a little easier than getting a new one.

When it came time to leave for the airport, I was struck by my excitement. I had been to Saturn twice and to the moon, but this trip to Italy was so much more...right. I had planned for this trip, but the trip across the Solar System had been sprung upon me with no planning, choice, or even a hint of expectance on my part. Being in control of my own trip made a world of difference. Little did I know, but there may have been some control issues going on here as well; I just wasn't aware of it at the time. I think someone was watching out for me.

Chapter 24 - The Tournament

I had only been outside the United States twice before - once with a church group on a mission trip to Mexico, and once when my wife and I were married. We had taken our honeymoon on a cruise ship to Jamaica, which also stopped at Cozumel, Mexico, and at the Cayman Islands.

But I had never flown on such a long flight or on such a large airplane. No, wait. Mr. Temm's spaceship had been bigger than this Boeing 747, a lot bigger. For that matter, I actually had been on longer flights than this, come to think of it. It's funny how the perspectives shift into focus if you stay on one planet.

My son Mark had never been on an airplane, however. He had never been out of the country. He was visibly excited to be going on this trip with just Dad. Because he had turned fifteen, there seemed to be no stopping him. His energy was all over the place, and his Taekwon-Do was very good. I believed he would be better than me someday, but he was going to have to work for it. He had already become able to score a few points on me when we sparred together in class. He had always loved the sparring aspect of Taekwon-Do most, but I had always loved the patterns, so we were each able to allow the other to have his way, and I like to think any competition between us came down to friendship. I felt lucky that my own son was also my friend.

We had to stop in Frankfurt, Germany, on that long flight. And then we had a four-hour wait in the airport there. I remember the German employee dressed in a military uniform as he stamped our passports and let us pass through customs. It seemed odd to be in a foreign land. I wondered if the military man spoke English, but we never really needed to talk to each other as he checked our documents. I was very aware that I couldn't speak German as we continued to wait at our gate area. I assumed the people who passed by would not have understood me if I had tried to talk to them. I bought us a couple of cans of soda from a vendor in the airport and realized too late that I had spent about three times what I was used to paying back home. I had some trouble understanding Deutschmarks and Euros and how they converted to U.S. dollars.

We would have been traveling with Mr. Halyard and the other students from our Taekwon-Do school in Texas, but we had decided to have a few days extra in Venice before our tournament started. We flew to Venice from Frankfurt on a smaller airplane. When we landed, it was interesting to me that our plane stayed out on the taxiway and we stepped out from the plane outdoors instead of through a gateway, as I had always done before. As we walked across to the airport buildings, I was glad it wasn't raining. My first impression of Italy, at the airport in Venice, was somehow not what I had expected. It seemed too casual and almost primitive or nonchalant. The facilities were fine but somehow just not like we had back home. Nevertheless, I liked it. I could get used to this.

We traveled by boat after that. Our hotel was in the vicinity of the famous San Marcos Square, and the whole Venice scene was everything I ever could have imagined. The armed guards and policemen we sometimes saw were rather daunting to us, but our smiles didn't seem to bother anyone.

I made the mistake of walking into a men's clothing store a bit too hastily. The man in the store sent us off quickly, I think, because we weren't wearing suits and ties or something. His Italian was beyond my understanding, but his temper and attitude was as clear as crystal. But I did buy a couple of Italian silk ties at a more tourist-friendly store.

We never rode in a gondola, but if my wife would have been there, who knows? Mark and I did visit one of the famous glassblowing factories and saw the exquisite workmanship. Souvenirs were rather expensive, but you have to bring things home when you travel abroad. I wished that I could have brought even a rock from Saturn home, but that whole subject was to remain a secret.

We got to walk across the famous Bridge of Sighs as we toured the museum.

We finally arrived in the city of Rimini by train from Venice. We had gone by way of Bologna, and I had especially liked the food there. Rimini was on the coast of the Adriatic Sea, and we did visit the beach once before Mr. Halyard arrived with the other seven students from Texas. The beaches in Galveston and Padre Island, back home in Texas, were on my mind as I looked out over the Adriatic, trying to remember what country was on the other side. I believed it was once called Yugoslavia.

It always bothered me when I could not speak the language of the people around me. I had to try and find a person to translate for us or just hope for the best when conversing with waiters and hotel employees. I often just couldn't understand something, so I had to accept the results without complaint. When our restaurant bill was over 60,000 lire, I had a little trouble following the conversation of the hostess. She wanted me to use my credit card because I would get a better price, due to the foreign exchange rate. But I never really understood why she was insisting I wanted to use my credit card. Later I figured it out, I think.

Even before our friends from Texas had joined us at our hotel, we had seen teams of Taekwon-Do students from other countries in the area. There were a lot of hotels along this part of the city of Rimini, and various Taekwon-Do groups were staying in all of them. In the hotel where we were staying there were groups from Scotland and Australia. I never did know if they had us three English-speaking groups together on purpose or if it was just coincidence. But I could scarcely understand the English spoken by some of those Scots, anyway.

It seemed that all the countries represented in the Taekwon-Do tournament had team jackets, so the various groups were always colorful and easy to identify. As we walked to the arena where the tournament was being held, each person carried his own gear bag, while many other groups walked alongside us. The groups of colored jackets must have been a sight for the local Italians. They probably didn't see foreigners in colorful groups like this very often. I heard there were almost a thousand competitors at that tournament from over forty countries. Imagining the languages, the customs, and the stories that could come from that group of a thousand martial arts students was boggling to my mind.

My son competed in the tournament on the first day, and he did well. His patterns were good, but the student from Malaysia won in Mark's first match. I was eager to see him fight in the sparring competition. That was his strong area. And in order to avoid a parent's bias, I will just say that Mr. Halyard told Mark he had never seen him fight better, even though he lost to the Russian boy. As it turned out, that same Russian boy went on to win the silver medal, so Mark was not too upset. He had done well against what turned out to be a champion.

My time to compete came the next day. I was only competing against eight other people, so I felt like I had a good chance to win. Apparently, there were only eight of us men over thirty-five who weighed over eighty kilos, if I remember the numbers right. But my first round was a bomb. I had to do *Ko-dang* pattern right from the start and failed to remember all that I had recently learned. At one time near the end of the pattern, I stepped with my left foot instead of my right, and that was all it took to lose.

However, I fought three rounds of sparring matches and won the bronze medal in fighting. The two-minute rounds seemed awkward and clumsy, but I scored big with the hook kick and the twisting kick. I think people don't expect those two as much. Most people seem to throw a lot of turning kicks and always with the same leg. I tried to learn from my mistakes, and I think I learned more from the matches I lost, funny how that works.

I was unable to break boards for any standing in the competition, but I did receive a medal of a different kind. Master Titus was there, of course, and he was the main judge of the power breaking competition. The Italian officials placed about nine boards in the big metal board holder, and each competitor would attempt to break them. No one actually broke his whole stack of nine, but someone from Norway broke four of them, so he got the gold medal.

When it was my turn to attempt the break, it felt like the whole world was watching. And it seemed quieter than any time I could remember. I stepped up and made a noise of my own by slamming my heel against that stack of boards, and it *was* loud. But none of the boards broke. However, Master Titus knew me, called me by name, and said, "Demetrius, if you would have kicked about an inch and a half lower, you would have broken those boards."

I was thrilled because the Master had taken the time to speak good words to me in front of the whole world. That was my gold medal.

There was a lot of fun, and a lot of worthwhile education on that trip to Italy. Mr. Halyard was coaching us along when he could, but he was busy with the U.S.A. Team events, and he won a gold medal in sparring himself. His wife had their two little girls in tow, and she looked a bit distressed at the work she was obliged to do. Bringing little ones over the sea was more difficult than she had hoped for, I suppose.

We all made new friends in various countries, and I got to wrap the American flag around my shoulders as I stood on the podium to receive my bronze medal. Mr. Halyard was one of the reasons we got to hear the "Star-Spangled Banner" in that arena. And there was a lot more, but I don't have time to tell it all here. Perhaps you will get the opportunity to attend an International Tournament someday. I highly recommend it.

As we left the tournament arena that evening, I had no idea that I was about to fall smack into a horrible nightmare of unwanted adventure. Little did I know that I would be leaving Rimini, Italy, in a hurry.

Chapter 25 - Chaos

That night, I was roused out of my sleep by a whistling and a sharp vibration on my left arm. I sat up straight and made myself remain calm until I had all the facts. Mark was still asleep, and I hoped I wouldn't have to wake him. I had a strange feeling that something serious was up, because my wristwatch was telling me that Monty had some news for me - urgent news.

I was able to see clearly enough to read the text on my watch's display. Monty had sent a message reading, "Chaos in Texas. Return now. Camry outside." I hoped this short message was an overreaction to a false alarm, but I had to check it out. I wasn't sure what those last two words could mean. Surely the Camry wasn't here in Italy, was it?

I checked on Mark and decided he would sleep soundly for a few minutes while I stepped out of the room. I put on my robe and grabbed the cell phone on my way. I would be able to call Monty and talk to him without looking suspicious, but Mark was not supposed to know about Monty and the Camry. And I was hoping I wouldn't have to wake him. I hoped that this would be an unimportant, insignificant chaos.

As soon as I stepped into the hallway and closed the door on my son, I called Monty on the cell phone. "Monty, what is the problem?"

"Mr. Adrien, there is a visitor from another planet wreaking havoc in your neighborhood in Texas. I recommend that we go straight there so you can take care of the situation before much more damage is done. The Camry is parked outside your hotel."

I had trouble believing this. It broke too many rules. I didn't want it to be true. But I ran down the stairs and went outside. It was after 2:00 A.M.. It was Italy. It was raining. There was the Camry, parked in a No Parking zone, right in front of the hotel. I must have stood there with my mouth open for too long because Monty's voice came to me from a distance, and said, "I recommend a quick departure, Demetrius." I had lowered the phone as I ran, and the voice came from there at my left side, where I had forgotten about it.

I snapped it to my ear and said, "Monty, who did you say is in Texas? What kind of damage is he doing? How did you get here with no pilot? What about my plane tickets?"

I was a bit excited, as you can well imagine.

"There is an alien creature, much like the one we destroyed on Dione, doing great damage to the houses in your neighborhood. I believe some people have been killed and injured. I have decided that the importance of this situation from a galactic political perspective must override my injunction to desist from flying the Camry without a pilot. The price of your plane tickets may not be refunded, but I believe you would agree that the dollar amount is unimportant in this situation."

Some people had been killed? And injured? I paused only shortly to consider all this, and I ran back into the hotel. We had to get our luggage, and we had to leave. Now. I had to wake Mark.

All the chaos with Monty and the rushing to understand and the rushing to get the luggage together and repacked: all was nothing compared to the one hateful fact that ate at my soul. I was going to have to get my son, my innocent son, involved in these darn alien encounters with weapons and missions to save planets and unknown dangers. I was never as angry in my life as I gently shook my son awake and revealed my nightmare to him. He was going to have to go with me.

"Monty. I have to bring my son with us, and I know you are not allowed to reveal yourself to him under normal circumstances. This time you need to put aside that programming and work with me, even though Mark is with us." I spoke as we rushed down the stairs, each burdened with our gear bags and luggage. Mark was looking a bit confused, and I had ignored his questions about what we were doing and where we were going. But he tagged along and kept up with me.

Monty's voice was not excited at all. "No problem, sir. I understand."

We piled the bags in the trunk and got in the waiting car. I didn't have to tell Monty to go; he took off down the road before I had even shut the door. It was surprising how quickly we got out to a remote area and took off into the air. Mark was thinking he was going to sleep in the car, I suppose, when he realized we were leaving; but when we took off into space, he lit up and remained very alert for the duration. I was getting the full story from Monty, so Mark didn't say much. He was taking in way too much, and I hated the thought of putting him through this. But I had no choice, of course, or so it seemed at the time. Maybe I should have left him with Mr. Halyard. I could have. Some of his friends were in the group from Texas. He would have had a great time traveling back with the group. But here we were.

It wouldn't have mattered.

Monty didn't have much new to tell me, he could only repeat the same news to me again a few times. I'm afraid I didn't listen well to Monty anyhow.

He had to tell me everything again later. I was too distracted imagining scenes of chaos. I was glad it only took a short while to get back to Texas. We could go at an incredible speed, thanks to the GAC, which kept the forces of rapid acceleration and deceleration from tearing apart the vehicle with us in it.

We landed in the street in front of my house, and I was appalled at the destruction all around. It was still morning here, and the sun was up. It looked like a war zone, with spent bombs and bullets in the streets. My house was damaged greatly, but still standing. However, the neighborhood houses as far as I could see were destroyed. Some were burning, but it was not the fire that had done the damage. It looked like bombs or missiles had blown holes in each house, block by block. Rubble and smoke surrounded us. I noticed there were no sirens, and there were no people.

I would have expected people running, sirens screaming, and human noises of many kinds. But there were none. This was definitely an alien scene. As I tried to understand this mess, I paused long enough to look at my son. We were out of the car, and he was looking at me now. His eyes were not asking me, "What happened?" His eyes were asking me, "Where are Mom and Michelle?"

I ran to the house, but it was too late. The alien who had caused this mayhem appeared walking out of my front door. He was eight or nine feet tall, and he was dressed in a military uniform with medals. He had a tail. He looked like a crocodile, to me, walking upright on his two hind legs.

Chapter 26 - The Lizard

The big, ugly creature had a big, ugly gun in his right hand. I noticed the hand had claws on each finger of different lengths. The gun was huge and heavy. I had to believe this was the weapon that had caused the damage all around me. I knew it was not an Elixir energy weapon like I had encountered before. Elixir electro-proton rays would not have made this type of destruction.

My fears were for my wife and daughter, but I heard nothing from the house to indicate their presence. Maybe they weren't home, and the monster had become mad. I felt that he must have been looking for me or he was looking for my family in order to get to me. I didn't have time to think how he may have found my home, but it did seem odd to me that it had taken over two years. I had just begun to believe this space alien business was over and done. I had just left an international Taekwon-Do tournament in Italy.

Now I had to get out of this big mess, which was probably my fault. What had I done to bring this upon my innocent neighbors? Where were the sirens?

The creature did not have the gun pointed at us. He was looking toward us, and suddenly stopped when he saw me. He seemed to know who I was. I thought I detected a smile appear on his face, but that was not a smile I would believe. My cat often looked like he was smiling, but do animals really smile? I had to wonder why this animal in front of me was wearing clothes and carrying a gun. Animals didn't do that. I hoped I wasn't going to ever get used to it.

He growled a great laughing roar and then looked at me as if I was supposed to respond. He looked at my son, and I saw something resembling satisfaction in the lizard's eyes. When he looked back at me and I remained silent, he let out a coughing breath and searched for something in his pocket.

I noticed he moved the gun to his left hand so he could use his right hand to reach into the pockets of his neat military clothing. So, he was apparently right-handed. He sat back on his massive tail as he stood there. The two legs and the tail together made a foundation for the standing position of this creature.

He pulled out a box resembling an old transistor radio. He fiddled with some buttons on one side of it with his claws. He used the claws like delicate tools. Each of the claws had a different shape and function, so he had two handfuls of diverse tools. He had cradled the gun in the crook of his elbow so he could use both hands to work the small buttons on the box. He held the little box up as if showing it to me, then he growled some more.

When he was finished with his series of growls, he stopped and waited again. This time the box spoke, and it was in English. It translated what the reptile said so we could have a conversation. "Am I privileged to meet the contort, Demetrius Adrien?"

I had no idea what a contort was, but it sounded like the word "pervert," as far as I was concerned. I did not think this dude wanted to make friends with me. He had an arrogant laugh. He waited, and when I did not answer, he adjusted the controls on the little box. "Do you understand me?"

I spoke to him, assuming his box would translate my speech for him. "Yes, I understand you. What do you want?" I thought it best to act ignorant.

The crocodile turned his little box toward himself, and I heard a growling sound come out of it. The monster looked at me and gave a short laugh. The box translated it as a laugh in English, but it wasn't very good. "Don't pretend you're not the contort that killed my brother. You have Elixir tainting all inside your house and on yourself. There is no Elixir tainting anywhere else in this whole sector of the galaxy, so why try to hide?"

I said, "So what do you want?" Actually I was afraid he would point his gun at us and fire at any time, and desperation was gnawing at the back of my mind. I wanted to step in front of Mark and protect him from this foul being.

He answered, "I want to see if you are as tough as your bragging. If you are, I will not only let you live, but I will let you travel with me as my serv-...companion. We can gain a lot of wealth and power if we combine our resources." I wasn't sure the transducer box was working properly because I had never bragged to anyone about being tough. I also wondered what resources he supposed I had. Perhaps he knew about my training for the Saturn mission with Mr. Temm. That training had made me a special specimen of the human race. I had better senses, better reflexes, better speed, and more strength than any other earthling. I also had a great database of knowledge in my brain. And I had Monty. Those must be my resources. But Monty's Camry could not travel across the interstellar gap, so I would not be able to travel outside the immediate solar system in that vehicle.

I needed time to figure out what to do. I needed to stay calm. I had to think. If I could distract him and perhaps overpower him, get his gun away from him.... "Before I can accept your proposal, I need to know what you have done with my wife and daughter. Where are they? If they are harmed, I may have to refuse your proposal and provide you with the Earth consequences of your rash actions here in this neighborhood." I was making this up as I spoke. It occurred to me that this was possibly not the same as talking to an Italian waiter. This foreigner may not know what secrets the laws and cultures of planet Earth might hold.

He and I had come a little bit closer to each other during our conversation, so I was on the alert for tricks. Right there in my front yard, in front of my ruined neighborhood, we were already mentally sparring, and I thought it might get more physical if we kept this up. I was acutely aware of that weapon, now back in his left hand while he held the translator box in his right.

He listened to my answer as it was translated, then he told me, "Your mate and offspring are not here. I admit that if they had been here, I may have killed them in my anger. You have caused me great trials in the past twenty-seven months as I looked for you. When you were not present in your home, I became a little upset." He gestured at the destruction he had caused, as if it were my fault. After waiting for the translation, he added, "You have no choice in the matter. You either die as payment for murdering my brother or you come with me and live, but only as long as you cooperate."

So, here is where things got out of hand. Perhaps if I would have gone with him, I could have eventually escaped and solved all these problems in a different way. But, I decided to be human again, and I suppose I insulted the beast. Having found out that my wife and daughter were not involved in this catastrophe, I was so relieved. I became a bit rash myself.

I had noticed that this reptilian man was a bit sluggish when he moved. I wasn't going to let that fool me because I knew that alligators and crocodiles could move quickly at times. However, it gave me an idea that I might be able to outpace his hopefully sluggish reflexes if I used surprise in my delivery. My plan was that he would not know what I was doing and would therefore not respond in an efficient manner. It was risky, but I had been scanning the area around me, and I thought I detected dead bodies in the neighbors' bushes. Risk was inevitable. This sparring partner was a murderer. Desperate action was necessary and fitting for this scum. I had no choice.

Perhaps I should have done this differently, but here is what I said: "Sorry, I would rather die than cooperate with a beast like you. I believe you are going on the path to certain judgment and destruction, and I will not go with you." I said this politely and with a smile, so it was his turn to wonder if the translator box was working. He took a moment to answer.

You see, my crazy plan was to surprise this guy with a Taekwon-Do technique called the midair kick. It was done with a full circle spin and was very powerful. It also would allow me to get a kick high enough for this tall opponent. It was a kick with my right foot, but I had to first step forward with the right foot, then as I stepped forward with my left knee, turning to the right as I jumped, I would finally bring my right foot into the air. Yes, I would step, jump, and kick, with the same right foot. Then the spin would carry me around full circle to kick with all my strength, straight toward the wicked creature's throat.

But one thing sort of messed up the situation, and, well, here's what happened. I hate to think of it, but it can't be helped now.

Before I heard the answer to my last comment through the translating box, I began my spinning kick technique as the beast was bringing his gun into play. I don't know who had the best reflexes or who had the fastest speed, but he was moving his left hand up to shoot as I started stepping to kick. My quick movement through the air toward the crocodile-man took me out of the line of fire, and my foot hit the gun on the way in. I still succeeded in breaking something in the creature's throat, and he fell with a great choking, gasping, growling exclamation I never heard translated.

But the gun had fired. After I landed on my feet and saw the result of my kick lying there in a reptilian, twitching heap in front of me, I turned and saw my son. He was down, and he was dead.

Chapter 27 - Escape

I was in shock for more than one reason. And then I heard the sirens. I had to run away from the sirens. There was a dying alien creature here in my front lawn. There was a dead body, *my son*. No, there were a lot of dead bodies. Hadn't I seen them in the bushes? I had to escape from this neighborhood, from this planet.

The Camry was parked right behind me in the street. But I had to do something. My mind was racing in many directions, and my body had to follow one of them. There was a way to solve all these problems. I started feeling a grim hope developing in my heart, but I was desperate to get out of here. Where was it? I needed the alien creature's spaceship

It was not too far away. In fact it was in my backyard. And it was also in three of my neighbors' backyards. It had crushed the wooden fences separating all of our backyards. I ran up to it and hoped I could fly it. But I couldn't even get in the door.

I ran into my house, or what was left of it. I was maddened and saddened to tears when I saw the destruction of the furniture and of my family's possessions. I think that lizard-beast had purposely destroyed many of the things in the house. Clothing, towels, portraits, and even light fixtures, were strewn around as if deliberately tossed and smashed.

I found the laptop computer still intact in its docking port. I think the outer casing of it was indestructible, and though scratched, it seemed functional. I grabbed the cell phone from its place on my belt and called Monty as I heard the sirens approach closer. "Monty. I need you to help me pilot the alien's spacecraft. What can you give me? Quickly, please!"

As I spoke, I was using the remote control buttons on the Camry key ring. There was a universal setting for opening any known lock in the galaxy. I hoped that the friendly people who had designed this feature had known about the type of door lock on the reptilian space vehicle. I pressed the buttons, and the locked door of the spacecraft slid open. It opened into a ramp that I ran up straight away. Inside the ship, I soon found the switch to close the door, sealing me inside. Now I had to find the controls and fly this thing away.

The first problem was seating. There was nothing like a chair here. I wondered how a crocodile would sit, and I reasoned that they probably wouldn't. The tail would be in the way. The ceiling was rather low, but that was unimportant. I found the cockpit, or what must be the driver's control board. It was on the wall under the windows at the front of the craft, just as you would expect. But there were no chairs. In fact, it looked like the whole board was at floor level, and I would have to operate things by laying down on my stomach. Weird.

So, that's what I did. I lay down on the floor like a lizard. Apparently, this was the correct position, because I found that the floor was contoured and padded like a couch for alligators. From here I could see out the front windows and had a very good view of the police cars, fire engines, and ambulances turning into the neighborhood. I opened up the laptop and set it where I could refer to it next to the dashboard, and I spoke to Monty.

He knew a lot of information about vehicle controls, but he did not have this particular model in his database. It was from a planet unknown to the Friendlanders, who had programmed Monty. Nevertheless, Monty was able to guide me when I described the setup to him. He gave me as much detail as he could from what he knew, which included diagrams, text, and three-dimensional holographic displays I would be able to utilize after Monty was out of range. Yes, I was planning to travel out of Monty's range. I needed to find Mr. Temm, and the Camry could not go where he was.

Monty had also given me everything he could to help me use the scanners, the communication system, the weapons targeting systems, and life support systems. I had a lot of general training of my own that would apply to the piloting of this craft, but Monty gave me some extra help to overcome the problem of reading foreign control labels and readouts if they were not translated into my language.

But they were. I was glad to discover that this alien spaceship had a translator built in with some of Earth's languages. Once I selected the English option, all the controls were a breeze to figure out. I remembered that little box the alien had used to translate our speech while we sparred in my front yard. I wished I had one of those when I was in Italy. It was a bit scary that aliens from distant stars, especially nasty aliens, could get so much data about Earth so quickly. That creature must have uploaded these languages as he approached our planet. He may have been in the habit of wreaking havoc on innocent planets, and it helped him if he could speak their languages.

It could have been humorous to see the looks on the faces of those policemen and emergency assistance team members, when they saw my spaceship take off from the backyard. It could have been, but it wasn't. I was in no mood for smiling, much less laughing. I had no concern for those people and what they might think of seeing a real spaceship. This was no UFO for me. It was my *life* right now.

As I flew the ship out into space and became familiar with the way things operated for lizard spaceships, I eventually calmed down and considered my situation. This was a serious business. I had my usual regrets as I thought of alternative ways I might have handled the situation. If only.... But I soon gave up the self-inflicted punishment of regret and thought of my wife.

It was Sunday. She and Michelle had gone to church that morning. That was why they weren't there to meet the crocodile in uniform. They would come home from church and find the whole neighborhood in shambles, and they would eventually find out what happened to Mark. I could not bring myself to just be sad about it. I had to be angry also. Thinking of my wonderful son, whose life was cut off in a horrible death, was too much for me to bear. And it was going to be even worse for my wife. I had to fix this. I knew how to do it.

Finding Mr. Temm was probably a near impossible task, but I had some ideas about how to do it. I spoke to Monty on the cell phone, which was open since I had first called him. "Monty, I need you to give me the best estimate of the direction Mr. Temm's ship took when he left the Earth's moon. Please keep in mind that he would probably have gone as far from his home planet as possible." Mr. Temm was desperately afraid that he and his crew were cursed as a consequence of their disobedience to God, and he did not want to take any of his new sinfulness back to the innocent people on his planet of origin, Friendland. I was silent as I waited for Monty to answer, but soon his calculated trajectory appeared on my laptop screen. It showed a line of the most probable exit from the Solar System and spread out as it fanned out to the most probable areas Mr. Temm would search. Okay. This gave me somewhere to start.

With Monty's help, I set up everything for the interstellar jump to the most likely star, and then I spoke to Monty. "I am ready to take the jump to the first target, Monty. I guess this will be good-bye until I return."

"Yes, Demetrius. Please be careful."

"Thanks. Do you know anything about Elixir tainting?"

"Not specifically. But I can speculate with some certainty that it is some effect of the Elixir radiation you encountered on your second trip to Saturn. You may remember how we came so close to the energy blast. I cannot detect the tainting myself, but the reptilian alien is apparently able to do so. I would think that the tainting was perhaps instilled into the metal objects you had in your pockets and clothing. Perhaps it is in your bones and teeth, as well, as indicated by the alien's conversation with you."

"Monty, what did the alien do when it arrived at the house?"

"I was aware of the creature as its vehicle approached from space earlier this morning. Your wife and daughter were gone from the area, as you know. The creature first looked into the garage where the Camry and I were located. He may have taken readings to verify the Elixir tainting, for he did not stay with me long. I read that he entered the house and thrashed around before he came out. He was enraged and loud, and he fired his weapon at the houses adjacent to yours, causing great destruction. I left to summon you in Italy at this point, but you can tell what occurred by the extent of the neighborhood destruction. And when we returned, he had been back inside your house, perhaps searching for some lead to help find you or your family."

"Monty, why do you suppose it took so long for the police and other emergency vehicles to respond to this attack on my neighborhood?"

"I believe it is possible, Demetrius, that this alien had superior technology that allowed him to thwart the alarms or somehow delay the communications warning the authorities. He probably jammed all the telephones and other signals that would have revealed his activities. It was a very complicated task by Earth standards, but not unlikely for an interstellar traveler, especially one who had something to hide."

It was good to hear Monty's robotic voice put the pieces together. I started to feel like I had a purpose again after the chaos. I was set to perform yet another mission. I was eager to leave for the distant star I had chosen, but I had a lot of questions for Monty. I was regretful that I would not have him with me this time.

"Hey, Monty. Before I leave, can you tell me one thing?"

"Sure, Mr. Adrien. What would you like to know?"

"What is a 'contort'?"

"That term applies to someone who distorts, or contorts, the time continuum for the illegal displacement of objects through time. I believe it is a derogatory term."

I already knew it was a derogatory term. I went ahead and said my goodbye to Monty and took off across the interstellar gap toward Mr. Temm and hope. But then it occurred to me what Monty had said: the *illegal* displacement of objects through time? No one had told me it was illegal.

Chapter 28 - New Friendland

I had some time to rest and even sleep on my first trip to another star. I am not going to try to explain the science of the jump across the great distance between stars. It involves some concepts the human race on Earth may never learn because our ability to discover it may be related to the curse of sin. When Adam and Eve ate that forbidden fruit, they caused a lot of changes.

But even without those changes, we had limits. Everyone knows that a person cannot be in two places at once and that we have to wait for things to happen. That sounds so trivial and simple when I write it that I wonder if you understand. What I am trying to say is this: the fact that we have time at all is a limit we must endure. As difficult as it may be to imagine, I suppose God does not have to wait for things. Anyway, the speed of light was one of the limits. Einstein and other scientists have discovered that nothing in this world can travel faster than the speed of light. It also appears that the speed of light is not like other things, in that it always travels the same speed, no matter where or how you measure it.

Imagine if you stood in a railroad car and threw a ball sixty miles per hour toward the front of the train. Now consider that the train was moving forward at sixty miles per hour also. But if someone standing on the ground next to the train were able to measure the speed of that ball, it would be going 120 miles per hour, the speed of the train plus the speed you threw the ball. That's easy to figure. But light doesn't work that way.

You might think that if my Camry was moving at just under the speed of light and I turned on the headlights, the speed of those light beams might be almost twice the normal speed of light. But it wouldn't. Believe it or not, the measuring apparatus would measure the light speed from my headlights to be exactly the same speed of light as always measured, which is about 186,000 miles per second. That comes to about 670 million miles per hour. But nothing, not even the hi-beam headlights from a high-speed vehicle, moves any faster than that finite number.

It's a great mystery that God created on purpose, for his own reasons. Personally, I don't know how any scientist can observe these things and not believe in God. What other explanation could there be except, "God did it?" It's just my opinion, and you don't have to agree with it.

But there is a way to jump the great distances between stars. That's the part that's hard for me to explain. The easiest way I can think of to help you understand is to say that the galaxy is full of a lot of things Earth has never seen, and among those things are some that travel faster than the speed of light. So, the scientists of some other planets have been able to observe the phenomenon, explain it, and reproduce it.

Here I was, traveling at the speed I needed to get to a distant star and have a nap along the way. I hope that's enough explanation because my head hurts from having used too much math during a career as a structural engineer for fifteen years. I think the mathematics needed to understand space travel between stars uses something that makes tensors look simple. Even though I know what a tensor is, I have never used the concept to calculate anything. Vectors, rather than tensors, work fine for my class of mathematics.

As I traveled, I remembered there was going to be a great amount of discomfort for a lot of people on Earth, especially in my neighborhood in Texas, if I didn't do something about it on this trip. There would be a terrible panic about aliens from outer space, about extraterrestrial murders and abductions, and possible political cover-ups, not to mention the scientific experiments with the lizard alien's dead body. I assumed he had died. What if he wasn't dead? That would be a whole new trouble. He might even escape and follow me. I wondered if he could follow my Elixir tainting, whatever that was. Apparently my body had received some change from the Elixir radiation I encountered a couple of years ago. Monty said it was probably in my bones and teeth.

Maybe Mr. Temm would know what to do to erase the tainting, if that were possible. I was counting on Mr. Temm to answer a lot of questions and to help me with the solution to the alien lizard problem. I feared that he might not want to help me. Besides, he was probably dealing with a whole new set of problems himself since I had last seen him and his people. His wife would have had their baby by now, and they would have built some sort of community and be living in reasonable comfort. They had such advanced technology and science, I imagined they could build a city very quickly. And they had the whole history of Earth to help them if they wanted to copy our type of system. They had been studying Earth for years before they called me to help them.

Maybe I shouldn't bother Mr. Temm after all. He didn't need me to interfere in his life, I supposed. I hoped he would be glad to see me at least. But I was committed now. I had to at least try. I was afraid Mr. Temm would not want me to attempt my solution, but once I explained how these new problems on Earth were direct consequences of my last mission, maybe Mr. Temm would share some of the responsibility. Surely he would understand that we have to go back and prevent this latest development. Perhaps it would be as easy as traveling back in time to early Sunday morning and being ready to meet this militant reptile at my house before he started wrecking the neighborhood. It seemed easy. I had done something like it before; I needed to do it again.

But maybe Mr. Temm wouldn't have any time machines to spare. Maybe he was unable to use that technology in his new circumstances. Maybe I would never find him on his new planet, out there among the stars. I had to try.

As it turned out, I got fairly lucky. I only checked three planets before I found Mr. Temm. That was more amazing than I realized at the time. The odds were astronomically against my finding Mr. Temm. I think somehow I was guided to find him. I will say this, however: I had fervently prayed to God to help me find Mr. Temm while I was flying to his star. That may have been why it worked. And besides, I should have prayed before I set the course for that first choice star. Perhaps God answered preemptively and helped me set the course before I asked him to do it. I know, prayer is a complicated mystery.

In any event, two of the candidate planets I chose were orbiting the first star Monty had suggested, but they were both too hostile for our kind of life, and my sensors showed me that they were uninhabited. So I had had to jump to the next star, and that's where I found the new planet home of Mr. Temm and his people. I went around the planet at a safe distance because I did not want to be mistaken for a hostile party. Mr. Temm would probably recognize my ship as a lizard craft and prepare to defend himself.

I opened a communication channel and spoke to the dashboard. "Mr. Temm. This is your old friend, Demetrius Adrien. Please respond. I need your help." I realized I was not well versed in radio communications, so I added, "Sorry, I got this alien spacecraft from a hostile visitor to Earth. It was the only way I could get here. Please respond, my friend."

There was no answer for a long time. Perhaps there was no one monitoring the equipment. Maybe they didn't even pay attention to the communication station anymore. My sensors showed that my transmission had been acknowledged by adequate receiving hardware, but that didn't mean any person had necessarily heard it.

Then I heard a welcoming voice. "This is Gabe Common. I have met Mr. Adrien, but I would like more confirmation of your identity. Please respond to the following question: Which is more valuable, two strips of black tape or a gold watch?"

I had to smile even though I was not in the mood. I had forgotten that friendship makes one smile, and I was visiting friends. I said, "The two strips of tape are much more valuable than any gold watch. But I have my Black Belt now, maybe you didn't know." There was another long silence.

The next voice I heard was Mr. Temm's, and it was a good sound. "Hello, Mr. Adrien! Welcome to New Friendland. I never thought I would see you again, but I am very glad now that you are here. Please accept our landing instructions and pardon us for the delay. It has seemed like a wise thing to check thoroughly the identity of all those who visit. We are getting too good at being careful, I am afraid. It causes us to be a bit rude and disrespectful to those who are indeed friendly, perhaps."

"Don't worry about it. I'm glad you are taking precautions. I'll see you shortly." I vaguely wondered if they had received other visitors besides me. That seemed unlikely, but I was new at this space travel thing.

I landed the alien lizard craft and sprang out to meet Mr. Temm and his wife, Ravsen. They were smiling, but it looked as if two years had changed them too much. I had no complaints, however, as we greeted one another. I also met Mr. Common and some others as well. They were more friendly now than they had been when I had been transported so suddenly to their spaceship, over two years earlier. I attributed their changed attitude to the fact that they all knew English, but they were changed more than that. Their nature was now different. They had a gusto I almost envied.

The new home for Mr. Temm and his people was a beautiful garden planet. There had been docile animals and birds all over, but no intelligent people. And so far they had not encountered any hostile or even carnivorous animals. It was a planet the size of Earth, and they had only begun to explore it all. I imagine they already knew a lot more about this planet, however, than our early explorers ever knew about Earth. I imagined Mr. Temm's technology was good enough to count all the birds on this planet from a distance.

But the touch of these human creatures had begun on the forests and hills of New Friendland. I call them human, but the greenish blue tone of their skin showed that they were definitely not from Earth. They had indeed built a community of houses with roads and sidewalks. They had water and electrical power supplied to every home. It was a lot like Earth, but perhaps not like Texas. But it was not like Italy either. This was a small town and seemed quite adequate for these few people.

Mr. Temm's spaceship had had a total of forty-eight people when I visited it a couple of years ago. With Ravsen's baby and maybe a few others, there would be around fifty people here. Whether they would ever become a populated planet or not, only the future would tell. I think they had a good start.

As it turned out, I had arrived in Mr. Temm's community in the evening, and the dinner hour was already over for the people. But Mr. Temm escorted me personally to his own house, and I met the baby. He was not yet two years old, and his name was Demetrius. I had almost forgotten that Ravsen had informed me that she was going to name him after me. It was an odd moment as I looked at little Demetrius. It had been a sad memory, as so many good memories are, to think back on those days when the Friendlanders had discovered their own corruption. They had sinned for the first time and were going to have to live with the consequences like the people of Earth. These two years must have been a struggle to accept the reality of death and other discomforts.

They had never had death as a part of their history. Because their Adam and Eve never disobeyed God, they had never been punished. The people of Friendland had never lost their pure relationship with God. Instead, their walk with God had been strengthened, and the evil one had been practically banished from their planet.

But some of them learned to travel to the planets and stars. Those led by Mr. Temm had traveled, perhaps for centuries, visiting stars and planets, gathering data from all the suns and worlds they encountered. Eventually they found the Earth and stayed there to study it for what turned out to be a long time. They were fascinated and at the same time repulsed by the sinfulness and death of Earth. It was foreign and new to them, so they stayed longer and longer, absorbing the data of Earth's history. They learned of war and weapons, of hatred, of scorn and deception. But they also learned about courage, gifts, loyalty, and sacrifice. They learned about laws, honor, disease, accident, murder, and insanity. They learned it all. And they learned religion too.

The God that had created Friendland, whom these people knew so well, was the same God who had written the Bible for Earth, the God of Abraham, Moses, and Jesus. They read about the Revelation of the Apostle John and the coming of the end of the age when all sin would be paid for. They learned about forgiveness.

Demetrius did not know why or how they sinned, but he knew how to help them when they did. Mr. Adrien led Mr. Temm to get his own personal forgiveness from God, and then Mr. Temm brought his ship's crew to the same forgiveness in each of them. Now they were all right again with God, but the cost was real. Now these forty-eight people would die when their age caught up with them, but they were still alive for now. Just like the men and women of Earth, they had to die. But the same forgiveness was there for them.

Of course, God had to withdraw from the close proximity they were used to having him. This would allow free will and faith and love to be possible. Mr. Adrien knew that God was there, but it required faith to believe and follow God. This forgiveness and reconciliation with God was the meaning of life on Earth, and now Mr. Temm's world had it too. It was no wonder that Mr. Temm would not go back to his home planet. He could not risk taking sin to a sinless world. This new home would have to do.

Chapter 29 - Business

The next day I had to begin my pleas for help. Mr. Temm and Ravsen were much more like Earth people now, so we had breakfast together, much like you would have at home. The foods were similar to our normal breakfast fare because the farm animals here on this planet were similar to Earth's animals, or Mr. Temm's people had brought their own animals, which was very possible. Maybe they had some chickens and goats with them. I never asked.

The Friendlanders had managed to make a large farm complex of modern buildings and facilities for the keeping and breeding of the various animals and for harvesting crops and dairy products. Because there were only the fifty or so people here, each doing his part, the task of feeding everyone was not too difficult.

I was eager to speak with Mr. Temm, and he suggested we take a walk through the town. I began to tell him the story of what had happened on Earth, but I soon realized that Mr. Temm did not know about my second trip to Saturn. So I started over and explained that story as well. He was attentive and serious as he listened to me. As I finished the story about my escape from my own planet, my tone of voice had some bitterness and resentment in it.

Then I said, "My idea is to go back in time and redo the scene with more thorough preparation. I can have a weapon with me and show up at the house before the reptilian beast shows up, and I can destroy him before he does any damage." I waited for Mr. Temm to respond, but he was thoughtful for a minute as we walked.

"Demetrius, your idea is certainly a plausible one, but let's consider a few things. What spaceship did you think you would use to travel back to your neighborhood on Earth? If it is to be the one you arrived here in, then you will have some problem finding a place to land and a way to conceal your alien craft from observation. Have you considered these details, my friend?"

"Well, no, but I *must* find a way to accomplish this. I didn't travel all the way here just to give up and go home. You can help me work through the details, can't you? First, we need a plan, and then…well, I had hoped that there might be some technology that I was unfamiliar with that could help me. I don't know if you have any more space vehicles you could lend me or if you could even build me a new one. Maybe you could transport me there without a vehicle. If my idea is not feasible, then, please, help me find a solution."

"Of course I will help you. Demetrius, my friend, I am still deeply sorry that I have caused you so much trouble, and I will not abandon you now. We will do something to get your son restored to you and your neighborhood made safe again.

"But there are some things I must tell you about that will have an effect on our plans, things that I have learned in the last two years." Mr. Temm stopped walking and turned to face me. "Demetrius, I am afraid I am going to have to apologize to you for another thing I have unwittingly done."

I had no idea what this new thing could be. I also realized things were not so simple as I had imagined they would be. But as we looked at each other, Mr. Temm eventually smiled. "We will find a way to take the necessary steps, perhaps one at a time. Before I explain my need for the apology I have referred to, I want you to consider another aspect of your time travel idea. Have you considered that destroying this new alien, as much as he may deserve to be destroyed, is possibly only a temporary solution? He may have another brother. Or perhaps there is a whole crowd of vengeful brothers and sisters from the same place these last two reptilian beasts came from."

It was true. I had not considered that. If one alien creature could find me, then another one could too. "So, am I destined to run from these beasts for the rest of my life?" I was thinking I might never see Earth again. I wondered if I could stand to roam the galaxy, running from every alien ship that resembled a threat. I would grow old out there in space somewhere, running forever.

"No, I think we can work something out. I will supply you with a time displacement module, and I will provide you with a way to get back to your home without being detected. Your real problem is the tainting of the Elixir radiation. Removing that from your body and your other possessions is impossible, as far as I know. The tainting is a subatomic phenomenon that cannot be expunged easily. The best solution to your problem will be to collect all the tainted items and destroy them. Their destruction must be complete on a subatomic level. I recommend a matter conversion to pure energy, much like the EMC feature of your cell phone.

"You must destroy every single coin, every key, every metal item that can be discovered to have the tainting. As difficult as that may be for you to accomplish and as imperative as it will be to do so, this still does not solve the problem."

I knew what he was getting at. "Of course not. Even if I succeed in destroying everything tainted in my house and clothing, it won't be enough. I have the tainting in my own body." The lizard had told me that, and Monty had confirmed that it was probably in my bones and teeth.

"Yes, but there is hope. Your body is constantly rejuvenating the cells of your flesh and bones. You have a high metabolism compared to other humans after the treatment I gave you two years ago. I believe the tainting will be gone from your body in less than five more years through the natural process of biological growth."

"Five years is a long time to wait. Is there no way to cover the evidence or maybe prevent the tainting from being read by alien sensors, maybe a shield of some kind? I would only need it for five years." I was feeling desperate again and wanted to keep fishing for possibilities. But Mr. Temm had little else to offer. He was more confident than I was, however.

"I believe it is unlikely that another beast is going to try and find you until the peers of this last reptilian creature receive word of his failure. And because it took over two years for him to find you, it is not likely that anyone else will be able to find you any faster. This is especially true if you reduce the magnitude of the Elixir radiation tainting in your household. By destroying most of the tainted metal items, for example, you will greatly diminish the strength of the tainting, and it will be much more difficult to read with any sensor." This was hopeful, but I was still not convinced.

Mr. Temm saw the despondency in my face, so he added, "Keep in mind also, Demetrius, that it may take years before anyone misses the alien creature back at his place of origin. Add those years to the time it would take a new creature to find you, and you have plenty of time for recovery. I think you have great hope of a peaceful future."

It seemed like we were avoiding the mention of the possibility that the destructive lizard alien may have sent my exact location back to his home planet. Maybe my phone number and address was now in some Galactic Phone Book in a thousand languages or more. I wondered, how much hope did I really have?

Mr. Temm and I had more planning to do, and though it was not a cut-and-dried solution, it was the best I could do. The important part was that I was going to get my son back. And the neighbors who had suffered and died were going to be restored to life. All I had to do was go back in time to early Sunday morning and be ready with a weapon. Because Monty had a record of the event, I would know the exact time and location that the beast was coming, and I would be able to overpower him easily. Then, once he was out of the picture, I could remove his spaceship from my backyard. Mr. Temm had some ideas about how to do that, but we would decide on that issue before I returned to Earth.

And finally, I would have to start destroying, by direct matter-to-energy conversion, all the objects in my house with Elixir radiation tainting. Mr. Temm would supply me with a sensor device capable of determining which objects those would be. I pretty much knew that it would be whatever metal objects had been in my pockets and any metal parts of my clothing while we were in close proximity to the Elixir blast from Dione two years ago. We had flown alongside of that lightning bolt of Elixir radiation for a good while, and though I was protected from the dangers of the blast, we were not immune to the tainting. Mr. Temm was considering giving me a new vehicle and a new talking computer. I could call it Monty if I wished. I would have to think about that.

So, the plan was set for the fixing of past dreadful memories. All I had to do was succeed in performing a relatively simple task. I had done such things before. I could do this. So why was I so nervous and depressed?

Chapter 30 - Cops

I stayed on New Friendland for another day because Mr. Temm had some things to tell me. Little did he know that he was going to answer some of my questions before I asked them.

As we walked through town that morning, we stopped often so he could show me the various facilities of the new community. The huge spaceship was parked near the town, as it had a lot of the most important facilities for life within its walls. The ship's laboratories, communications, weapons, sensory, and other systems were all very much a part of what made things work around here. The vessel's nuclear energy supply was going to last through many generations of New Friendlanders. The ship could still be used to fly into space, but that would require a lot of disconnecting and reconfiguring of things in the town to enable the community to get by without the ship's facilities. But it had not lifted off for any flying since they had first started digging in two years ago.

Mr. Temm had things set to provide as much security as possible to the whole area where the people ventured, which included many acres of farmland and future farmland around the town. They had built three tall towers to hold security sensor equipment well above the trees and hills, and new towers could be built as needed. If any spacecraft flew into the space around this stellar system, the receiving station would know it and would send alarms to the various leaders of the community directly in their homes or to the personal communication devices they carried.

"I would imagine you don't receive very many visitors here. I don't think Earth had any space visitors in its entire history." I was actually joking because the sighting of UFO's was a very real thing to a lot of people on Earth. And, besides, Mr. Temm had visited the moon and studied Earth for years. Who knows how many alien people knew about Earth without earthlings knowing about them? And I knew that a certain reptilian alien had visited there recently.

But it would have been strange to have an alien visit Earth in an official capacity with an open purpose and interest in meeting the people. Most people on Earth didn't believe there were aliens on other planets. I suppose that was because the ability to travel to even the nearest star was nothing but a dream without new technology.

But he informed me, "We have twice had visitors since we have been here. One was from a man like us who was merely traveling and the other visit was from the police."

I was stunned. "The police? Which police is that?" I wondered if Mr. Temm was joking, and I half expected him to deliver the punch line next.

But he explained. "There is an organization called the Galactic Police Force. We learned more about them from the other visitor. He warned us that they were coming. These police officers were looking for someone who had broken the law, but the description of their query was of someone unknown to us. They were pursuing a person of insect ancestry, but we have never met any such creature."

I had difficulty believing this story. It was a bit too much for me to take in. I think it was not so much that I refused to believe it, but that I wished I didn't have to believe anything more. There were going to be too many people in my life to deal with if this trend kept up. I didn't want to believe that the galaxy could be so populated. I wanted to be from the only planet that mattered, and Mr. Temm was reminding me this was not the case.

"The police officers had become aware of us as they approached, and they stopped to visit us, but there were other issues that they informed us about. It is common for the Galactic Police Force, also known as the GPF, to come across planets with unknown populations. So, the GPF policy has been to make records of the newly found civilizations and attempt to fit them into the jurisdiction of the police force. Basically, we were invited to join the Galactic Conglomeration of Planets.

"However, because we number only forty-nine, they were more interested with our home planet than us. I tried to be elusive and honest at the same time, but, alas, I am afraid there may be trouble for our family back home if the police ever make it there. Mr. Adrien, I am often overwhelmed with grief, and these new things add to the burden of my despair. I do not want to be responsible for the evitable troubles of other people. But I must try to live a useful life, and continue."

He was perhaps feeling that the police were unable to understand the difference between these forty-nine explorers on New Friendland and the people of their original planet, Friendland. But there was a great difference, a difference inside the heart and souls of each of the forty-nine people. The policemen likely considered Mr. Temm and his small group to be colonists who represented a greater population on their home planet, and so any political or legal dealings would have to take place with the government of the home world, not with these interstellar explorers. But they were wrong. Mr. Temm had no intention of ever communicating with his family back on Friendland. I wondered if he had been compelled to reveal the exact location of Friendland to the police, but I didn't ask him.

Instead, I wanted to ask a different question. "Who was the *first* visitor you had? You said he was a man like us. Tell me about him."

Mr. Temm seemed glad to change the subject. "He was a little bit mysterious, but that can be attributed to his personal modesty or sense of privacy. We were glad to give him what he may have needed on his travels, but he had no real needs. We offered him food, fuel, and whatever supplies or parts he may have needed, but he refused all but a single day's accommodations. I think he was just looking for a friendly face to visit with."

Mr. Temm was silent for a moment, as he considered something. Then he continued. "The man was also mysterious for another reason. Mr. Adrien, he spoke about *you*. Do you have any friends traveling among the stars in this sector?" Mr. Temm had a gentle smile as he asked me this because he knew the answer to his own question.

"No, of course not. But surely he was not from Earth, was he?"

"I don't think so. He seemed to know all the details of modern interstellar space travel and was quite comfortably suited to his position as a pilot. He had a simple but adequate vehicle, and he apparently understood as much as we do about technology and science. But our conversations were few, and, of course, I did not pry unnecessarily into his privacy."

You can imagine that I was eager, if not impatient, to find out what this mysterious visitor may have said about me. How could anyone from another planet know anything at all about me in the first place? "What did he say about me?"

"He had already told us, with a hint of warning in his voice, that the police were coming this way. He told me not to tell them about you. His exact words were, 'I strongly recommend that you say nothing whatsoever to the police officers about Demetrius Adrien.' This man, who gave his name as Luke also said that 'Mr. Adrien will just be hindered by these unnecessary cops.'

"Luke was rather elusive in his speech and refused, although politely, to reveal any more information about the matter. I will say, Demetrius, this man called Luke had a strong effect on us in a way that is difficult to explain. But when the police came, I remembered his warning, and I never mentioned your name to them. After all, I did not expect to see you again, and the matter seemed unimportant then. Seeing you here now, even though I am thoroughly pleased by your visit, causes me to rethink the significance of all these coincidental visits. Perhaps there is trouble brewing, and we should be on the alert."

It was unusual to hear Mr. Temm speak with any urgency. He had never known words like "alert" until he studied Earth and learned our ways and language. He and his people did not have any words related to time issues, like haste, hurry, and quickly. The fact that people did not age and die on his planet was the reason for this apparent lackadaisical attitude. Now he had an urgency, which had been foreign to him a few years ago. But he had aged visibly since then as well. They all had. I had.

Mr. Temm told me that the man named Luke had spoken about some other things. He was very informative to Mr. Temm about the Galactic Police Force and the Galactic Conglomeration of Planets. Mr. Temm had been impressed that Luke was trying to educate him for some reason, almost as if Luke himself had some interest in these galactic political issues and wanted to spread the good news.

And yet, this good news was something to beware of. Mr. Temm had been struck by the hints of warning with which Luke had flavored his information. The gist of the message was, "You need to know about these police and these galactic politicians, but be wary of them at the same time."

Mr. Temm did eventually tell me his apology, which he had alluded to earlier. I had been prepared to write it off as insignificant, whatever it may be. Surely Mr. Temm had given me so much benefit in our previous encounters that anything he may feel the need to apologize for must be unimportant. But when he told me, well, I must admit I was somewhat surprised. At first, I did not know how to react.

"Mr. Adrien, my friend, I found out from Luke that the time travel you have done is illegal. I have caused you to be guilty of a serious crime. Although I am apparently not legally guilty of any crime, I consider myself just as guilty as you because I practically forced you to break the law. I can plead ignorance of the law, but that does not excuse me, and it does not belay the consequences."

I wasn't sure how big of a deal this was at first. I sort of wrote it off, as I had intended to do all along. But then I realized that Mr. Temm was deeply concerned in his greenish expression. More concerned than appropriate, I thought. I felt that he was leaving something unsaid, so I urged him on. "Are the police looking for me?"

"Oh, no. They described the person they were seeking as an insect with wings and three compound eyes. He would measure about four feet tall, or perhaps you would say four feet long, and resemble a dragonfly to us, I understand. I have no idea who that creature may be or what he has done to get the police chasing him.

"Demetrius, the crime of time travel is a capital crime, punishable by a fate worse than death because of legislation by these galactic politicians Luke told me about. Apparently, these people have been trying to form some sort of galactic empire for many generations. However, they have accumulated only a few star systems as members, when you consider the size of the galaxy.

"However, their power is real, or so Luke said. These police officers are military soldiers of a formidable army. And if they capture a person who is found guilty of distorting the time continuum for the purpose of displacing himself through time, as you have done, they imprison him in a timeless continuum that may last indefinitely. I will do everything in my power to keep you from such a fate. Mr. Adrien, you must see my need to apologize to you as I have never apologized to anyone in my life. I am guilty of causing you much grief."

I waited in silence for a while. "You are my friend. You had no intention of hurting me. You have given me more than anyone has ever given me. Don't worry about apologizing. We just need to do what we need to do, like we planned. Let's get on with it!"

I detected some relief in Mr. Temm. Either he was glad to get this information off his chest or he was glad I was not mad at him, or both. But now he sighed before he responded to me. "Mr. Adrien–"

"Call me Demetrius. You're my good friend."

"Thank you. Demetrius, I have some hope that perhaps these wild stories from a wandering space traveler may not be true. There is certainly some possibility that all this is nothing to worry about after all. But Luke was right about one thing. The police did come soon after he left, just as he said they would. But that doesn't necessarily mean that everything he said is to be believed."

He was ready to end this conversation, but I had to ask him, "Mr. Temm, why is it that you have these time travel machines, yet you say you are not guilty of the crime of time travel?"

"Yes, I do have the capability of committing the act of displacement through the time continuum. We learned it directly from our Creator, God. It seems a long time ago. As it happens, more by coincidence than by decision, I have never transported myself or any other person through the time continuum besides you. I have always moved products and equipment through time, and that is not illegal."

I asked him, "Why would you ever want to move such objects through time?"

"Oh, there are many reasons. If a customer needs a supply of product right away but I don't have it in stock yet, I can still promise to deliver it to him that day at a specific time and a specific place. I can then wait a week if needed, either to acquire the product, or to let it ripen in the case of a fruit or plant, or I can have it modified before I send it. And then, even though it may be a week after the delivery time, I can send it back in time to the exact time and place that we agreed. It is a complicated business and involves some manipulation of the merchant. And payment often does not come when I expect it. Needless to say, sometimes it is better that the customer not know the details of my methods."

It sounded like Mr. Temm had had a good handle on deception and manipulation long before he met me. I wonder if he learned it from the Earth people, or somewhere else. But I didn't ask. It was none of my business.

"Well, I guess I'm going to earn my title as a contort, because I have every intention of going back in time again if you still want to help me."

Chapter 31 - More Plans

I was ready to get going on my new mission. I *needed* to get going on my new mission. I did not want to sit around too much and think about my troubles. I had to make myself sit and listen as Mr. Temm went over all the details with me.

He was not going to have to train me the way he had before. That previous training was still quite sufficient for the piloting of the spacecraft back to Earth. We had agreed that it would be best to make use of the same ship I had stolen from the defeated reptile, but now it would be equipped with a time displacement module, much like the one my Camry had before I dismantled it.

I asked a question then that turned out later to be a very important one. "When did you make this time machine? Do you keep a supply of them around here or something?"

Mr. Temm was going over some lists in front of a toolshed with one of his acquaintances, Gabe Common. They were conversing in English, but I think it was a bit awkward for Mr. Common. He didn't have the fluency of the foreign language Mr. Temm had. And I knew that the English language was considered difficult to learn by foreigners.

So, Mr. Temm answered my question casually as he continued working. "This one was made at the same time as the one we gave you, over two years ago. Whenever we take time to accumulate the materials for an important or unusual piece of equipment, we try to stock up and make some extras, to save effort later. We made five of these time displacement modules at the same time."

As I watched them working on equipping of the lizard spacecraft, another thought crossed my mind. But after I asked the question and then heard Mr. Temm's response, I felt that I had opened a subject that may have been a bit tender. I had asked, "Where is Mr. Chamm? I'll bet he would be helpful in this type of work." I had met Mr. Chamm before but had never spoken with him. He had done a lot of the work on my Camry and had helped program Monty to be my servant and copilot.

But Mr. Temm's answer seemed a bit tense. "He and a few of his friends have decided not to join us here and have settled on another part of the planet. We have not communicated with him for over seventeen months now. He will not be helping equip you this time."

Mr. Temm seemed to reconsider, as if he realized that this would prove to be significant news to me, so he set down his clipboard and turned to me. "Mr. Chamm and I do not see eye to eye on some matters of leadership. We have his settlement under observation, but he shows no signs of friendship with us, whatsoever. I am sorry to have to demonstrate our lack of harmony, but it is now a simple reality."

The word "now" was added to remind me of the great change that had occurred to all of Mr. Temm's crew, including Mr. Chamm. They were now all sinful, and they were all going to die. I supposed he didn't like being reminded of that any more than we earthlings.

A lot of what Mr. Temm and Mr. Common were doing did not involve me, and I knew that my briefing would follow before I departed for Earth. I was therefore quite pleasantly relieved when Ravsen joined us out at the work field. She seemed more beautiful than I had previously thought, but the greenish hue of her skin left a certain bias in my impression. Looking at her now, I seemed to be able to see the beauty a bit better. I think she had changed in some way, within her soul, perhaps, that made her more interesting than she had appeared to me before.

Don't get me wrong. My wife was very often on my mind as the most beautiful creature on the planet Earth. Sorry, I need to upgrade my thinking: my wife was the most beautiful creature in the Milky Way galaxy. But as a scientist and an interstellar traveler, I was able to appreciate the beauty of Ravsen as she walked out to speak with her husband in the middle of the day.

She nodded to me as she walked casually up to Mr. Temm to ask him something. And after they conversed in low tones for a minute, she turned to me. I had been sitting in a chair off to the side, trying to study some of the text that was supposed to help me fly the reptilian alien's spacecraft better. I had found it tedious reading and not very helpful at all. So Ravsen's company was a nice break from the chore.

I stood up to greet her, and she smiled her return. "I have suggested to my husband that perhaps I could serve you lunch at our house. He has agreed that perhaps that would be a fine idea. Would you join me? We can walk together."

I told her I would be glad to accompany her, and I noticed that I was rather hungry. I had not been eating regular meals since I had left Italy. However, before we left, I glanced over at Mr. Temm. When he saw my eyes, he nodded with a smile. My duties as a field worker were expendable for a while.

As we walked to the Temm house, I asked Ravsen, "How is the baby?"

"Young Demetrius is doing well. He has begun his life with good health and good provision from the Lord." After a few moments, "There is a helper in our house who is tending to Demetrius while I am gone. You can meet Ms. Seffani when we arrive. She should have prepared lunch by then."

I had stayed at the Temm house the night before, but I had not seen all of it. Now I was escorted to a patio area at the back of the house. We had come in by way of the front door, and walking through the house, we made our way out by the back door. There was a roof over the outdoor area, and a lunch was set there. A woman, who must have been somewhat younger than Ravsen, was introduced as Ms. Seffani. Her greenish blue face wore a shy smile of youth, but the contrast of her black hair made her look quite grown-up to me. She had the small child in her left arm.

And there was the cat. I did a double-take because this cat was completely out of place, here on a distant planet. As I stared at the orange cat, who just sat there near the wall and looked at me, I was struck by the fact that this was *my* cat - our cat - the one we called Pixel, who had disappeared from my house when I had returned from my Saturn mission.

Strangely enough, both Ravsen and Ms. Seffani waited while I stared at the cat. They looked at me as if expecting something. Eventually I realized I was acting unusual. "Oh, sorry. Is that, by any chance, the cat from my house?"

Ravsen breathed a bit of a sigh, and then said, "Yes, but I was not sure if you would remember. I did not wish to bring grief to your memory, so I did not say anything."

She acted for a moment as if she was unsure of how to explain, or whether she should explain at all, so I spoke first. "Why don't we sit down, and you can tell me about the cat, if you wish. I'm just glad he's all right. I had wondered about him ever since I first noticed he was gone."

She began a casual conversation as we ate. "When Mr. Temm and I first began to live life in our newly changed world, we were very busy simply coping with our newfound salvation from a dreaded fate. And such details as the cat from your house did not receive much attention for a long time. But once we began taking hold of the details of our lives and the lives of our fellow travelers, we eventually understood that we had made a mistake concerning your cat.

"There was nothing we could do, however, because we honestly believed that we would never see you or Earth again. So we tried to make a good home for the cat. He has had his physiology trained and repaired so that he would be happy away from you and your family, as much as possible. I think he remembers you, however."

She said this as the cat rubbed up against my legs and made the old familiar purring and meowing sounds I still remembered this cat making. After two years, he seemed a bit more tame and laid-back. Ravsen continued her story, almost apologetically.

"When Mr. Temm and Mr. Chamm remade your house on Earth for your comfort and convenience, it involved, of course, removing the old house and then transporting the new one into its place. Any living creatures had to be removed before this process could take place. I am sorry, Mr. Adrien, but we were not familiar with the need for pets and domesticated animals. Even though we knew that many people on Earth kept animals as pets, we did not truly understand what the pets were for. So we did what we inadequately thought was the best thing. We let Pixel come with us instead.

"Now, of course, we understand the joy a cat can bring to a family. Little Demetrius loves his kitty." I was relieved, as well as surprised, to see the cat and was glad that he was alive. At the time of that lunch conversation, it had concerned me in the back of my mind, that my wife, daughter, and son had not noticed the missing cat. However, I never got to pursue that topic because another one came to me, rather suddenly.

As we resumed our meal, Ravsen surprised me. "Mr. Temm was hoping you would stay here with us instead of constructing your own house when you return. We have already added a small suite of rooms and facilities to accommodate you, if you would like to see them."

All thought of the cat flew away as I realized what she was suggesting. I didn't actually react with a choke, like I might have, because the reality grew slowly in my awareness as I replayed her words over and over. *When you return*.

After I destroyed the alien creature back in my neighborhood, I was going to have to go somewhere. I don't know why I never thought of it, but I was going to have a similar problem to the one I had had two years ago. If I destroyed the evil lizard creature before he did all that damage to my neighborhood and to my son, then Monty would never go flying to Italy to warn me. The Demetrius and Mark Adrien who were sleeping in a hotel room in Italy would go right on without being roused from their sleep. They would make use of those airline tickets. They would come home to the safe neighborhood. And where would *I* be? Good question.

Ravsen and Mr. Temm thought I would be coming back here to New Friendland.

I remember losing my appetite rather suddenly, and not because I was full. I had to make my apologies as I fled to go back and see Mr. Temm. I don't think Ravsen was upset. She probably had been confused by my behavior ever since she had met me, and this was nothing unusual, I suppose.

But Mr. Temm had nothing much to add to ease my chagrin. He had said, "I am sorry. I assumed that you would not want to solve the problem this time in the same way you had solved it before. It may not technically be murder, but it is perhaps something like it, especially if you consider the point of view of the one whose life is being terminated. Do you have any alternatives other than returning here where you will be welcome? Please keep in mind also that you would be more difficult to find here by any aliens who might be looking for Elixir radiation tainting."

He had a sort of lecturing tone of voice, like that of a friend who cares enough about you to tell the truth. I think he was right, though; I wasn't sure if I wanted to convert another human being's body into pure energy just so I could have my way in the world or the galaxy. Perhaps I needed to admit that bad things happened to good people, and leave it at that. If I were to at least save my neighbors and my son - give them back the lives they deserved - well, I should be content to live a simple life here with these loyal friends after that. Perhaps they needed a friend too. I could be a useful part of the New Friendland society.

As I was resigning myself to these feelings, another inkling of an idea started to come into my mind. As I heaved a sigh of relief, I also decided I missed Monty. Maybe I would have him write the story of what he had done while I was gone, and I could read it when everything was back to normal.

Chapter 32 - To Sleep or Not to Sleep

I was about to leave to head back to Earth. On the surface of the matter, it was agreed that once I had gone back in time by the three days required, that when I returned to New Friendland after destroying the enemy reptile creature, I should move myself back into the future to arrive at a time after I left there. In other words, it would be awkward if I went back beyond yesterday to take care of this alien problem and then returned while Ravsen and I had been having lunch. It just wasn't necessary, and Mr. Temm was rather stern about that. Having a second version of me show up while they were preparing to send me off was just not acceptable.

The reason I said "on the surface of the matter" is because I had within me a couple of alternatives that I had not voiced to the others. My thoughts below the surface were not decided yet, so I was not consciously keeping secrets from my friends. But it was clear in my mind that I was going to have a time machine that could fly from star to star and that I might use it for something my friends didn't need to know about. Theoretically, I could still return here to whatever moment in time I chose, no matter how much time I actually spent running errands around the galaxy. If I came back with a long white beard, Mr. Temm might give me another lecture, but he couldn't do anything about it.

The thing that bothered me was the way we had it all scheduled, there were going to be two Demetrius Adriens in the galaxy. One would be living a relatively normal life with a wife and two teenagers in Texas after a nice trip to Italy, and the other would be living on a farm on the planet New Friendland with forty-nine people with greenish blue skin. The idea of both of us carrying on with our separate lives didn't seem fair. I would be the one who missed out. I would be the one with the short end of the stick, the raw deal, the smaller piece of pie, the worst of two choices. My counterpart on Earth would be the epitome of "ignorance is bliss." He would never know that I existed.

I considered asking Mr. Temm to erase my memory after I came back here to retire early. He would probably be able to change my brain so that I would never miss my wife, kids, and Taekwon-Do school. But that was just too much like cutting off a perfectly good arm. I could never do it.

Yes, I had been thinking a lot about possible alternatives.

Mr. Temm, Ravsen, Mr. Common, and Ms. Seffani, along with everyone else not in Mr. Chamm's group, gathered to see me off. Each of them, it seemed, had made a small speech or word of encouragement or thanks in English. It was touching to listen to the words. I heard a variety of degrees of fluency, and more than one of them did not really seem to speak English at all. But they all tried. I realized that if I did end up coming back here to live, it would be a very nice bunch of people to live with.

Mr. Temm and Ravsen stood together as I entered the spacecraft above them. "We look forward to seeing you soon, with news of your success."

I said, "Thank you," and then I shut the door. And as the silence of the sealed chambers of my ship surrounded me, I wondered just where I was going to end up, success or no success.

The ship now had a few differences about it. Mr. Temm and his friends had made some modifications. I had been told that the new onboard computer was as good as the Monty I was familiar with. They had managed to give me chairs to sit in so I no longer had to lie down like a lizard. This had been done by lowering the floor of the whole piloting area. The lowered floor had the effect of giving me more headroom. The air was less stuffy, and I had better controls for the pressure, humidity, and temperature now, if I wished to adjust them. But it wasn't until I left that I realized I had no music. It was too quiet. Oh, well, I could find some when I got closer to Earth.

One of my secret thoughts was about what to do immediately after I destroyed the lizard creature. Once that was done, and there was no damage to my neighborhood, I could travel a few hours further back in time and visit myself in Italy. Perhaps there would be an opportunity to safely eliminate the Demetrius there and take over his place in the family. Mark would never know I had been away for a few days, right?

But, of course, there was that problem of murdering innocent people and assuming they would understand, if they only knew the circumstances. Not likely. I tried to imagine what I would do if Demetrius Adrien walked up to me and suggested that he was from the future, and perhaps I would agree to letting him murder me so he could take over for me and have a better life. Somehow, I did not see how I would ever agree to that.

I wondered just how guilty of murder I might actually be already and how ironic it was that the police might be chasing me someday for displacing myself through the time continuum and not murder. How ironic that the crime I had actually committed was done in complete ignorance, but the act of killing another man was not even a crime in my case. At least, I assumed that it wasn't. After all, how could I be punished for killing a younger version of *myself*?

Maybe the Galactic Police Force had a way to decide these cases. Maybe I had already committed other crimes I never knew about as well. I found myself glad that the Milky Way galaxy was so incredibly big. I might need to stay hidden for a long time, like the rest of my life.

One of the problems that makes time travel so incredibly complex, requiring sophisticated computer technology, is that things like planets move a lot and they are not where you might expect them to be when you arrive there at a time in the past or future. For example, if I had a perfectly calibrated trajectory to reach the planet Earth programmed into my ship's guidance system but then decided to engage a time displacement system so I could arrive at Earth a year earlier, well, I would have to change the trajectory, because the Earth was not in the same location as it was a year ago. My beautiful, calculated trajectory would take me to a cold spot in outer space where no Earth had arrived yet, and I would be wasting my time in more ways than one.

Traveling only a few days back in time was easier, but the Earth, or any planet for that matter, would travel huge numbers of miles in just a few days. Most people don't realize that the Earth goes around the Sun at a speed of over 65,000 miles per hour. If you also consider the movement of the Sun within the galaxy and the movement of the galaxy among the other galaxies, the speed is quite overwhelming.

The latest time travel technology was able to minimize this awkward effect by adjusting something they called "the time origin of the space continuum." It's sort of like locating exactly where the Big Bang occurred and adjusting it to suit your needs at a given time.

Anyway, sorry to bore you with technical talk, but I thought some of you might like to know. But, as I have mentioned before, the curse that exists on Earth will probably make it impossible for us to ever discover time travel before Jesus comes back.

I had a voyage of many hours in front of me, so I tested the chair I was in by leaning back and stretching. It would serve well for some sleep. I checked all the gauges and made sure the trajectory was automatically set. The ship would fly as it had been programmed to fly while I slept, and I would be aroused by an alarm of one sort or another if anything unusual occurred.

But sleep did not come so easily. I had my decision-making mode in gear, and I had to think things through as I sat there with my eyes closed. The questions needed answering and were going to keep me awake until satisfied. The questions were not going away because they were first asked in my soul. And so it was on that voyage that I decided to have Monty write a chapter of my story. He would be able to tell it better than I ever could. My records of all that I had been through were always there in my journal, but he was the one with all the data. He not only had my journal on the laptop computer, but he had an enormous amount of data and sensory ability. I was sure he would be able to tell a fine story.

I reached out and started tapping the buttons of the laptop to give him something to start on. And then I made some adjustments to the ship's time displacement settings. I decided it was important to send a message to Mr. Temm about my schedule changes to our plan, but he would not receive it for a long time across the interstellar distance. That was okay. They would eventually get the message, and it would clear up any questions they might have.

The ship's configuration needed some altering for my newfound plan to work. I wanted to set a new course for the automatic pilot. And I made sure to set an alarm so I would not oversleep.

Once I was finished deliberately tweaking the program for my new trajectory, I sat back and found that sleep was finally easy after all. It seemed like I hadn't slept very well for a long time, and suddenly I was able to do something about that. I think I had a smile on my face as I slept, but I can't prove it.

Chapter 33 - Taking Arms

My name is Monty. I have served as the onboard computer in the vehicle of Demetrius Adrien ever since I was initiated. I have also been learning to assist him in the endeavors of his life. I will be telling you some of the details of his story in this chapter.

Let that suffice as an introduction because this chapter is not about me. This chapter is about Demetrius Adrien, just as all the chapters have been. Here is what happened.

Once Demetrius had instructed the onboard computer (whose name is unknown to me) to calculate and then initiate the lizard-alien ship's trajectory, he slept for a few hours. When the destination was properly near, the alarm sounded, and Demetrius awoke fairly well rested. He leisurely allowed himself to come to full consciousness, and then he deliberately ate a large and healthy breakfast.

When the time was right, he took the controls of the spacecraft and programmed a new trajectory. He seemed to perform all of his actions smoothly and slowly, but with precision. He appeared to have a joy in his expression as if he were glad to breathe the air, smell the aroma, and see the light around him.

He did not initiate the new trajectory, but turned his attention first to another part of the control panel at his far left. This was the control panel installed by Mr. Temm for the use of a new transport system, which had been added to the reptilian alien ship while it had been grounded on the planet New Friendland. After working the controls of the transporter and then again working the controls for piloting the ship, he rose and walked closer to the window that revealed the panorama of starry space to him.

He stood and looked around at all the sky on display there, and he eventually brought his eyes to focus on the nearby Earth. It was close enough to him that he could see the continents where people lived on the planet. He had caused the ship to orbit the planet in the particular location, which would allow a good view of Texas. He was going to go there.

After watching for a few minutes, he checked his wristwatch. Then he waited yet another minute before stepping to the transporter chamber. Inside the chamber was a small control panel, and Demetrius turned his attention to the buttons there. The chamber door shut, and shortly after that, Demetrius pressed a series of buttons and operated the appropriate dials and switches, then he stood still with his hands behind his back. He stood there quietly for a long time, possibly deep in thought. Eventually, he stepped back out of the transport chamber. He went back over to the pilot's seat and sat there, but soon he began to quickly type on the laptop computer again. After he was satisfied with what he had typed, he unhooked the laptop from its connection to the ship's computer, and he closed it. When he returned to the transporter chamber, he had his small laptop computer clutched to his chest, as if it were dear to him.

Shortly after that, he pressed the last necessary buttons of the control console and stood still again. A few seconds later, he disappeared as the transporter took him to the surface of Earth instantaneously.

Demetrius appeared in the backyard of his house in Texas. He stood there in the same position he had assumed in the transporter chamber, with his hands clutching his laptop computer. It was night. He listened. He sniffed the air silently. He turned his head from side to side, and slowly looked around in all directions. The wooden fences separating his backyard from the neighboring backyards seemed like new, fresh lumber. He could see the silver heads of the nails he himself had used to build the fence. The air was crisp like winter in Houston, perhaps in the mid-forties, Fahrenheit.

Demetrius walked quietly to the gate where he would be able to see out to the front porch of the house. He had to look through the narrow gap between the boards of the fence and the brick wall of the garage, but he was able to see the well-lit porch area. On the left was the access door to the garage, and to his right was the front door of the house. He set the small computer down on the pavestones near his feet. Demetrius was going to wait there, unseen by anyone who might pass by or even walk up to the house. From there he could see most of the front yard and all of the front porch. He could see the sidewalk and the street out beyond the yard, as well. But no one approaching would see him behind the wooden gate leading to the darkness of the backyard.

Demetrius knew that the Toyota Camry was inside the garage. He also knew that the Camry's onboard computer would be aware of his presence in the backyard. The vehicle's onboard computer would also have already known of his orbiting approach in the reptilian alien ship.

But the computer would do nothing to interfere. Demetrius Adrien had discussed this matter with the computer before. If the computer in the vehicle sensed that there were two Demetrius Adriens, it would just treat them both the same, unless some dilemma arose, such as conflicting orders from two directions simultaneously. Demetrius was not concerned with the Monty in the garage. He did not intend to cause a dilemma for Monty. That would not be necessary.

Demetrius knew that there was a second Demetrius Adrien inside the house, to his right, sleeping in his bed upstairs. He also knew that his wife and two children were away on a vacation. They were due to be picked up at the airport on Wednesday, and this was only Tuesday morning. He took his cellular telephone from the holster on his belt. To another Earth human being it may have appeared that Demetrius was about to call his wife in Seattle. That was not the case, however.

From the backyard, Demetrius was waiting for a third Demetrius Adrien to come walking up through the front yard. The third Demetrius would be approximately eight hundred fifty feet down the street at this time, and he would be here very soon. Demetrius looked at his watch as he stood in the dark behind the gate. The face of the wristwatch illuminated itself for approximately one second as Demetrius read the exact time. I believe Demetrius did not need to consult his watch to know the time because his ability to keep track of the seconds was uncanny for a human being of Earth. But the act of consulting one's watch is an Earth ritual that serves many other purposes besides finding the name of the exact present moment of time.

Demetrius became slightly tense as the other Demetrius entered the scene. This man who deliberately approached the house had Elixir radiation tainting in his bones and teeth. His pockets were full of metal coins and keys with the same Elixir tainting. The rivets in this man's blue jeans, as well as the metal eyelets holding his boot laces in place, also had Elixir tainting. His belt buckle had it. His wristwatch had it. His wedding ring had it. He walked as if he knew nothing of any tainting, or so thought the Demetrius who waited.

The hidden Demetrius placed his cell phone up to the gap between the gate and the garage wall, which he had been peering through, and pointed it at the approaching man. There was no need to wait much longer. The EMC feature of the phone would reach the distance. But there was a moment when the older, hidden Demetrius looked into the face of the other Demetrius, who was oblivious of any eyes watching. He saw that two years had made more difference than he might have thought. He saw some worry in the man's countenance, in his expression, which seemed to result from more than just this moment's determination.

But he pushed the final two buttons of the combination required to trigger the EMC, and the well-lit Demetrius Adrien on the front porch disappeared. His Elixir-tainted body seemed to curl in on itself and shrink immediately into a small, round marble of intense, dark energy, and then it disappeared entirely, collected and contained as energy into the storage pack of the cell phone. This ended the life of one of the three Demetrius Adriens and destroyed all evidence of Elixir tainting from his clothes, pockets, and body. Demetrius stood still for a long time, waiting for nothing.

Then he breathed an audible sigh. He opened the gate and stepped onto the vacant porch. After looking toward the front door of the house and waiting another long while, he retrieved the laptop computer and turned to the garage. He entered there without hesitation. If any other hand but his had applied pressure to that garage door, there would have been an alarm sounded to awaken the sleeping Demetrius who remained in the upstairs bedroom. This was a sleeping version of Demetrius who was going to test for his First Degree Black Belt in Taekwon-Do on Saturday. But the hand of Demetrius Adrien, the Second Degree Black Belt, was a friendly hand to this home's security system, and no alarm sounded.

Mr. Adrien knew that the younger Demetrius had not met the talking computer in his Camry, nor had he learned that its name was Monty. But as he opened the car door, he spoke, "Hello, Monty. I want to dismantle the time distortion device. Please provide access to the trunk and the toolbox."

"Yes, Mr. Adrien. You will find the access door open now." Monty's voice spoke quietly from the dashboard.

Demetrius had previously performed the job of dismantling the time distortion module and did not need any instruction to complete the job in twelve minutes. While he worked, he spoke briefly with Monty but showed very little feeling or emotion. He stayed intent on the work he was doing. He stopped only for a minute and put the laptop computer into position on the driver's seat of the car. With the car door open, he told Monty to download everything that was on the small laptop computer and retain the information for future reference. Monty would be able to do it without any hardwired connection.

As Demetrius resumed the job of dismantling the time displacement module, he also spoke to Monty as if in casual conversation. The task of downloading all the data on the laptop unit did not interfere with Monty's ability to converse with Mr. Adrien.

Finally, after completing the job, Demetrius hefted the components of the time travel device, picked up the laptop computer, and proceeded to walk away. He went out of the garage and headed down the road from where the Elixir-tainted Demetrius had come. Thus burdened, and appropriately destined, this Demetrius became aware of the Elixir tainting in his own body. He had not forgotten.

The alien reptilian ship stood empty and weightless in a stationary orbit over the Earth. There was no life in it, but many lights were lit, and some lights were blinking on and off. There was no sound in the ship's chambers. The seal separating the cool, clean air and the comfortable temperature of the ship's interior chambers from the frigid vacuum of space was utterly and completely moot. The ship's insignificant exhaust fumes fizzled into nothingness with perfect neglect.

Suddenly, but slowly, the ship turned, until it was pointing straight toward the Sun, around which the Earth had orbited since its creation. And then the craft shot straight ahead with tremendous acceleration. It would take only about ten minutes for it to reach that star and crash into it to be completely destroyed.

Chapter 34 - Separation

Demetrius Adrien walked toward the location of the Toyota Camry that was tainted by the effects of Elixir radiation. This automobile that had been to Saturn twice and had deflected a great blast of Elixir lightning would be the easiest source of tainting an alien sensor could read. Being made mostly of metal, the car would exhibit the telltale tainting throughout its structure and throughout the metal equipment it contained, including Monty, the talking computer. Demetrius walked steadily, thinking thoughts much like he had thought over two years ago, when he had walked the same path, but in the opposite direction.

He wanted to be distracted, to leave off thinking about whatever was coming next until it came. Perhaps he could think about the Third Degree Taekwon-Do patterns he would learn someday. They looked very cool. One of them had sixty-eight movements in it, but it was still not the longest one of all twenty four. He tried to recall its name. Of course, he was not allowed to learn that pattern yet. *Yu-Sin*, it was called. But, fortunately, Mr. Halyard pronounced the name like, "You shin," and not exactly like it was spelled in the manual. But getting his Third Degree was not going to happen for over two more years. There was a sleeping Demetrius in his house who was not even a First Degree yet. Demetrius walked on steadily.

He seemed to be drawn to think about what he did not want to think about. He walked faster. It was less than a mile from his house to where the Camry was parked. As he approached the clean, shiny car, he knew that the Monty inside would detect his identity and see that it was different than the Demetrius who had walked away an hour earlier. But Monty would know it was still Demetrius. This Monty knew about time travel, and Demetrius had spoke with Monty about the possibility of a second Demetrius walking up to it. Just like this.

He opened the rear passenger door and deposited the time distortion module from the Camry in his garage onto the back seat. Then he entered the driver's seat, closed the car door, and sat still for a few moments. The car was quiet, compared to the sounds of night he had just walked through. Sounds within and without his soul.

He said, "Monty, I have a change of plans for you. You won't be going directly to destroy yourself and this vehicle like we discussed a while ago. I may want to go somewhere first."

"That's fine, Demetrius." Monty's voice was robotic and unchanged from its usual tone, but Demetrius couldn't help feeling awkward that he was not really the same man whom Monty had last spoken with. From this Monty's point of view, Demetrius Adrien had gotten out of the car and walked away, only to return an hour later, but appearing to be two years older, and wearing different clothes. Monty asked, "Is everything all right?"

"Yes. Monty, how long would it take to get to another star in this vehicle?"

"The nearest star, other than the Sun, would take over six years to reach, Mr. Adrien."

"That's what I thought. I guess that's a little bit too long to wait. I suppose we had better stay more local then. Let's go!"

Demetrius started up the car and drove off into the night. And once he was safely out of sight of all onlookers, he took off and flew the car-ship manually past the moon and into a leisurely trajectory toward Venus. As he flew he did some programming to set a course for the spacecraft to run while he slept. It would accelerate the car up to almost the speed of light, but a sleeping pilot would not feel the motion, thanks to the GAC. Monty was aware of the programming Mr. Adrien was performing, even though there was no speech between them. Monty understood, in his mechanical way, where the trajectory would take them.

After having a thorough and slow look at Venus, Demetrius settled himself into the seat for more sleep. He had some dreaming to do. He did not set an alarm this time.

The version of Monty in the garage at Demetrius Adrien's home that Tuesday morning was able to sense that the trajectory of the Camry had slowed down to observe the planet Venus. The Monty in the garage was also aware of the sleeping Demetrius in the house nearby. He watched as the Camry left the vicinity of Venus and shot like an arrow into space, headed straight for the Sun. It was apparently not going to slow down for an observation of the planet Mercury on the way.

Monty was able to know that the Sun was rising early Tuesday morning, even though he was closed inside the garage. His sensors were very good. But as good as they were, he was not able to actually calculate the very small change in the Sun's brightness that occurred at exactly 7:48:32 A.M. It was too small, compared with the size of the Sun, and it was too far away. But Monty knew that the Camry with two time displacement modules and a sophisticated onboard computer had just crashed straight into the Sun at full speed along with the older version of Demetrius Adrien who had visited here so recently. He knew that another Demetrius Adrien was just waking from a restful sleep in the house next to his garage. He should be able to live a normal life from now on. He was going to become a First Degree Black Belt in Taekwon-Do in a few days.

The voice that came out of the dashboard in the garage that morning was not heard by any ears. "Bull's-eye!"

It was not meant to be heard.

The End of *The First Degree*.